Praise for Carolyn Cooke's

AMOR AND PSYCHO

A *Publishers Weekly* Best Book of the Year

"Cooke writes with humor and great affection for people, and she is unafraid to take on the inexplicable. Her willingness to follow her characters to places of mystery, wonder, pain and confusion makes the experience of reading these intense, remarkable stories a deeply empathic one.... In this book, where the forces of love and destruction are locked in constant battle, we can hope for Amor, but more often than not Psycho has the last word."
                                                        —*San Francisco Chronicle*

"Sex and death go hand-in-hand in [*Amor and Psycho*].... Cooke's wit and heart enliven ... somber material."
                                                        —*The Miami Herald*

"Carolyn Cooke's writing is addictive. Her prose is so compulsive and flavorful, you can almost feel it in your bloodstream.... Cooke's stories do not just confront realities: they grab them, pinch them, knead them, and then hand them over to the reader—who devours each story and is left with cravings for more."   —*Bustle.com*

"Cooke's stories twist and turn, playing games with language. They don't stop where you think they will . . . [and] they leave you with something: shards of phrases; a lifetime of attitudes conveyed in a word or an aside; or odd, perfect details that stick in your mind."

—*Publishers Weekly* (starred review)

"An edgy collection of powerful, engaging, offbeat stories. . . . The product of a mature and considerable talent."

—*Booklist*

"Cooke takes readers to various cultures and times to examine the anxiety, hopes, struggles, and, above all, the ever-present human quest for love and acceptance. . . . A definite page-turner."

—*Library Journal*

CAROLYN COOKE

AMOR AND PSYCHO

Carolyn Cooke's *Daughters of the Revolution* was listed among the best novels of 2011 by the *San Francisco Chronicle* and *The New Yorker*. Her short fiction, collected in *The Bostons*, won the PEN/Robert W. Bingham Prize, was a finalist for the PEN/Hemingway Award, and has appeared in *AGNI*, *The Paris Review*, and two volumes each of *The Best American Short Stories* and *The PEN/ O. Henry Prize Stories*. She directs the MFA writing program at the California Institute of Integral Studies in San Francisco.

www.carolyncooke.com

ALSO BY CAROLYN COOKE

Daughters of the Revolution
The Bostons

AMOR AND PSYCHO

Amor AND Psycho

stories

CAROLYN COOKE

Vintage Contemporaries
Vintage Books
A Division of Random House LLC
New York

FIRST VINTAGE CONTEMPORARIES EDITION, MAY 2014

Selected stories in this work were previously published in the following: "The
Boundary" in *AGNI Review*; "Isle of Wigs" and "The Snake" in *Idaho Review*;
and "Aesthetic Discipline" on Fifty-Two Stories with Cal Morgan (Harper
Perennial). www.fiftytwostories.com

The Library of Congress has cataloged the Knopf edition as follows:
Cooke, Carolyn.
Amor and psycho : stories / by Carolyn Cooke.
p. cm.
I. Title.
PS3553.O55495A46 2013
813'.6—dc23 2012045297

Vintage Trade Paperback ISBN: 978-0-307-74147-9
eBook ISBN: 978-0-307-96213-3

Book design by Cassandra J. Pappas

www.vintagebooks.com

Printed in the United States of America
10 9 8 7 6 5 4 3 2 1

For Randall Babtkis

Contents

AMOR AND PSYCHO

FRANCIS BACON

*I*n the early eighties, I often spent afternoons at Bob's House, which is what everyone called the twenty-thousand-square-foot Beaux-Arts mansion on East Sixty-seventh Street, said to be the largest private residence in Manhattan. There were always women there, always called "girls," and Laya looked like all of them to me—soft, fat, seventeen-year-old eager-to-please mouth breathers who signed their contracts with made-up first names and requested, for their take-out lunch, Classic Americans from Burger Heaven. Having grown up poor in a small town myself just three or four years ahead of Laya and her ilk, I felt the pinch of proximity as we strove upstream together toward what I hoped would become a vast gulf between these girls and me. Meanwhile, I lived in terror of being mistaken for one of them. To guard against losing my edge (I hoped to become a writer), I'd refused to take a serious job, preferring the professional twilight zone of the men's magazine industry. The vulgarity of the writing assignments didn't bother me; I imagined myself in the position of the Isaac Babel character in his story "Guy de Maupassant" and considered myself lucky that, with my English major and thirty WPM, I hadn't been forced to become a gofer at a fashion magazine. I also enjoyed Bob's blurred, autocratic presence, his white shirt unbuttoned to the belt of his sharkskin slacks, the chains around his neck, the long gray chest hair. His empire was worth $300 million that year; he was nearly at the height of his power to shock.

At that time, I needed little, apart from interesting experience, in order to live. While working for Bob, I subsisted on fancy lunches paid for in company scrip, and free cocktails and hors d'oeuvres at openings for artists the company knew.

My responsibilities entailed exactly what we were doing on this day: traveling across town to Bob's House, listening to Bob's orgiastic creative direction, then putting words into the mouths of Babes. Later, from a gray-carpeted cubicle on Broadway near Lincoln Center, I would create implausible erotic monologues (based on implausible true-life experiences) that suggested unspeakably childish innocence, the slight resistance one might encounter parting a raw silk curtain in the dark, accompanied by some subtle but binding statement of adult acquiescence. What better training for a writer than inventing little stories, arousing a casual reader with ordinary language thrillingly unspooled? The story arc was simple, sexual: foreplay, action, climax, denouement. Not that I supposed the men who read our magazine required much in the way of denouement; most of them probably closed the book once they'd spunked. The magazine took great pains—wasted—to expose corporate and government crimes and cover-ups. (We hated cover-ups!) We published the steamier fictions of Roth and Oates.

Working for Bob made me feel like a real writer, commissioned, dared: Give me twenty-four hours and I could give you a story about a lonely coed and a washing machine that could leave you breathless and satisfied.

Exposure to Bob's antiquities and follies had awakened my capacity for judgment. I felt contemptuous of every lapse in his taste—the carved marble toilets, the glazed fabrics, the white piano, the gallons of gilt. (My own shotgun flat, which I shared with my old college friend Mira, contained no furniture we hadn't plucked from the street. It was here in this studio, with its cold radiators and scuttling cockroaches, where I did my "real" work at night, brutally scribbling over fresh drafts of my austere prose poems.)

We traveled by taxi across the park to Sixty-seventh Street—an executive, a graphic designer, and a "writer." Inside the town house, we waited for Bob. We always waited; we waited for hours. It was Bob's dime; we were Bob's army, the pornographer's pornographers. Sometimes we waited all day while topless females cavorted with eunuchy-looking men in European bathing suits by the Roman-style swimming pool, which had been carved out of several venerable rooms. Or we sat in Regency chairs arranged around a fireplace whose panels contained decorative carvings of six-breasted women. Sometimes we waited until we saw Bob and his girlfriend, Kathy, dressed for the evening, descending the stairs and leaving by the front door. (Bob's face—before the cosmetic work—was sculpted into marble columns along the stairs, and the wall sconces that illuminated the way up to Bob's "office" were—or at least looked very like—molded testicles of glass.)

When we arrived, Laya—the girl-woman we were going to give away in a contest—was waiting, too, surrounded by the usual surplus of yellow-eyed men in their fifties and sixties, dyspeptics drinking seltzer water. One of these men immediately offered Laya a weekend in East Hampton. She slid off one strappy sandal, tucked a bare foot under her round bottom and leaned toward her interlocutor. "Is that on the beach?" she asked.

When she saw our trio, she lit up, as if she could have any idea who or what we were, and said, "Hi—I'm Laya!" The "creative team" introduced ourselves, then Ernie, the leering butler, appeared with a tray of vodka drinks. Laya asked for a can of Tab. From another room, or possibly some kind of intercom system, I heard someone say, "Put that nipple up again, or I'll have to come over and do it for you."

I resented waiting (dogged by the feeling that I had more important work to do), but Laya seemed to be enjoying herself the way a hunter enjoys oiling his gun, the way a whale enjoys breaching. We drank our drinks. Laya deployed her long hair as she turned the beam of her attention from one yellow-eyed man to the other. Stray bits of her monologue escaped, which I mentally filed for future use: "Capricorn," "unicorn," "nineteen," "calligraphy."

BOB EVENTUALLY SENT WORD via Ernie, and we ascended the stairway of faces and testicles. He stood for Laya, and took her hand. Bob saw himself as an innovator, an idea man, a feminist. He liked to establish this right away. "I've arguably done more to advance the status of working-class women than Betty Friedan or Gloria Steinem," he told her.

"Absolutely," said Bob's girlfriend, Kathy. Bob had met Kathy—a brilliant dancer with a background in finance and science—at a men's club in London in 1969, the same year he launched his magazine. Entranced by her beauty and talent, he had bribed his way backstage to her dressing room, where they discussed nuclear fusion. Now Bob and Kathy were funding a team of eighty-five scientists to "work around the clock" in New Mexico; Bob was investing twenty million dollars in a casino and a nuclear power plant. His seemingly unlimited capital came from profits from his magazine, where his innovations to the print centerfold had made him rich, rich, rich!

Bob spoke generally to the room, continuing his feminist theme: "We were the first to show full frontal nudity, the first to show pubic hair, genital penetration. We remain the innovators, the leaders. We pushed the sexual revolution forward." Bob looked the way he always looked—blurred, boyish, reddish and old, his white silk shirt unbuttoned to his belt. "You are all a part of it," Bob told us, spreading his arms to include Laya, Kathy, a few cretinous men, the "creative" department, even the paintings on the walls—the Picassos, the El Grecos. We were all a part of it.

One of the themes of his expensive art collection was, naturally, flesh—some of which I recognized from my survey course in art history. Bob owned a number of those fantastically macabre still lifes of Chaim Soutine, flayed rabbits and ducks hanging upside down, pools of blood spilling out among the crystal wineglasses, decanters and blood oranges.

But today Bob had a new enthusiasm—the painter Francis Bacon. I'd never heard of him. A Bacon leaned against a wall. We stood around it, looking down. In the center of the painting, a lone figure howled to the point of implosion. "Bacon," Bob said, "didn't paint seriously until his late thirties. You know why? He was looking for a subject that would occupy his attention. This is it. The figure. The *orifice*.

"Our magazine is inspired by these ideas. It's vivid and bold, and it's all about opening up the figure. I want a woman who does not simply lie naked representing a woman. I want to make photographs that immediately connect the viewer with the sensation of being in the presence of this woman. I am not interested in the woman; the woman means whatever she wants herself to mean. What interests me is the sensation produced by the photograph."

Laya looked studiously at the painting, as if it might teach her how to be.

Even Kathy's Rhodesian ridgebacks sniffed around the Bacon. Laya tripped on her heels avoiding one of the dogs, and Bob reached out to grab her. The canvas sighed and fell to the rug. One dog, quivering, escaped from beneath it. Bob picked the painting up and leaned it back against the wall. "Don't worry," he said, looking the painting over. "Art canvas. It's strong."

We sat, finally, at an oval table, overlooking a platter of raw meat artfully arranged around a bowl filled with toothpicks. Bob got to the point: "With all this in mind, I want to run a contest. Two weeks in Rio or Paris—someplace like that. Laya's the grand prize."

Kathy slowly raised a cube of meat in the air. The Rhodesian ridgebacks trembled with anticipation, then broke into competition.

Bob turned his soft, blurred eyes on Laya and said, "The contest will be tastefully done." Laya nodded encouragingly at Bob. Of course, of course, tastefully done.

My job, Bob explained, would be to help to shape the story in such a way as to eliminate any tawdry elements. Laya and I would spend an hour together in the "red room" in conversation, from which I would extract her adorable essence, her hopes and dreams, which would appear in the promotional material. One of the cretins handed me a press kit, which contained Laya's résumé, a high school report card, her height (5′2″), her measurements (35–22–35) and her ambitions: "too model and act."

Bob and Kathy left us to go have dinner at an Italian restaurant famous for its lewd murals and Neapolitan pasta puttanesca. After dinner, Bob and Kathy would stop by some wealthy industrialist's house for half an hour, as long as Bob ever stayed at a social gathering. He had a phobia about being kidnapped and held for ransom, and also he had little in the way of conversation. But this going out into the evening and coming home at nine or ten was one of the great things, I thought, about Bob. He did not hang out with the other porn kings. He lived and socialized right on East Sixty-seventh Street, and was rather abstemious in his habits.

INTERVIEWING LAYA WAS like being tended to by a friendly, paid person. We sat together in the red room with the sound track to *Last Tango in Paris* piped in like a gas. Ernie brought us cheeseburgers from Burger Heaven, still in their Styrofoam containers, which I resented, although I ate mine. Laya plucked at hers; it was too rare. She told me about Texas and, later, Arkansas, about her one-eyed mother and her generous and encouraging stepfather, about her scarlet fever and teenage rebellion, about her early talent as an artist, about being selected for a local car dealership commercial when she was only thirteen. She sat on her bare feet on the red silk couch and leaned toward me, flirty and confidential. "Tell me who, you know, who I should get close to. I almost know—I have ESP—but I can't trust myself because my spirit is so open."

LATER, after leaving Bob's House for the day, I met my roommate, Mira, and her new boyfriend, Amir, at the Russian Tea Room. We ate blini and caviar, and drank ponies of iced vodka and samovars of tea on Amir's expense account. Afterward, Mira went to the flamboyant penthouse with Amir (they called each other "Amira"); I refused a cab to maintain sobriety and economy, and walked home.

I stayed up all night writing Laya's "story"—about an ambitious and talented calligrapher with nonthreatening ESP who dreams of becoming an actress and discovers her sexuality at fifteen on a 747 to Rome. In composing, I entered a fugue state. I realized that choice and freedom are not necessarily optimal conditions for work, and that the most confining, restricting and repulsive situations sometimes open themselves up to be investigated, like the terrifying "orifices" within the "figures" of Bacon. From this black hole of desire that yawns within us all, I heard Laya's small, hopeful voice bubble up and simply wrote down what it said.

When I returned the next day to Bob's House with my story, I found Laya outside the red room, sitting at the white piano and playing "Baby Elephant Walk" to a swarm of middle-aged men who hoped to screw her. She wore a halter dress short enough to reveal a fresh hematoma on her thigh, and expensive gold hoops in her ears. Her hair had a metallic sheen. I thought of the way crows are drawn to foil in their bleak winters, and that this flirtation, which might lead to anything, to sex or marriage or death, was not a fantasy for Laya. It was the real life; it was what she did. She used her body the way I hoped to use my imagination—wantonly. She may have known already that the men she was flirting with could not really help her. They were sleazy, salaried men from Mamaroneck or Babylon, for whom the endless stream of young women like Laya—or like me, for that matter—was a job perk; many of them weren't even straight or single, just curious. Flirting with Laya, or having sex with her, was part of a fantasy or charade, while real life marched on in shadows behind the scenes.

Within a few years, many of these men would be dead of AIDS, caught and frozen in the common imagination by the stigmata of livid sarcomas on their faces and the backs of their hands. It was as if Francis Bacon saw that future wait- ing, named it in bright colors and abstracted figures, nailed it. Before I saw the Bacon paintings, I'd thought of the bar- rier between charade and real life as an ironic principle that young, attractive aspirants might transcend without much difficulty, like the velvet rope at the door of a nightclub. Imagine Laya, for example, who got everything she had come for—a small temporary fame made possible by men and her own amenable sexuality. (She became an actress, married a producer, lived for a period on a yacht off Skopelos, divorced, moved to London, and died at thirty-two, discreetly, of a disease she wouldn't name.)

That night, I read the tale—the fictobiography she and I had made up together—to Laya and Kathy and Bob. The three of them softened around the mouth as they listened and afterward said how beautiful it was. Bob said, "This is what I do—take a young woman of charm and talent and give her a chance to reach her potential." Kathy fed a cube of beef to the dogs and said, more pragmatically to Laya, "See what you can get out of it." (We often boasted of how the first black Miss America had profited handsomely from the exposure our magazine had given her.)

Bob showered Laya and me with scrip to the Copa, and I wantonly imagined the Veracruz snapper I'd command. Impossible to go to the Copa alone; I was more than ready to wait another hour for Laya, who continued to discuss details of the contest with Bob and Kathy and make new connections and arrangements with other men, working with more passion and intensity and for longer hours than I ever did.

While waiting for Laya outside the Roman pool, I flipped through a catalogue from a retrospective of Bacon's work at the Metropolitan Museum and read about how the artist squandered his time until he knew he could be serious, until he found a subject that could hold his attention. I studied photos of his London studio—the liquor boxes, the knee-high trash, the paint cans and brushes, the broken mirrors, the accumulation of thousands of images Bacon would pluck from the ankle-deep soup that functioned for him like an unconscious mind. The mess had a willful quality I admired; it excluded everyone but the artist himself, who had to work in self-imposed conditions that nearly rendered work impossible. Bacon's detritus boasted of his promiscuity, his gambling, the chronic messes he made by seizing every scrap of life that might serve his discipline.

I ripped a photo of Bacon's studio from the catalogue and laid it on the pile of company scrip. The scrip looked like play money—or like a child's certificate of achievement. We'd use it all, Laya and I—we'd eat and drink and make a little mess of the evening. With a fuzzy resolution born of several ounces of Russian vodka and a gnawing hunger, I promised the ladies of the multiple tits that one day I'd tell their stories, too. Sometime later, a dry finger touched my face with the slightest threat of a fingernail, as if I'd been chosen at random to play some brutal, competitive sport.

AESTHETIC DISCIPLINE

*K*arim Brazir was an artist and a bohemian—alluring, sexy, passionate in an intense but impersonal way; almost perverse, maybe even borderline somehow. His name rhymed with Karen, and in fact his parents, who interestingly misunderstood the name on a trip to Cairo and Istanbul, during which they conceived him, spelled it that way. He used to call me at night in New York and ask me in a gravelly voice to take a taxi over right away to his loft in a then-disused part of town. Romantic, I presumed. I'd push the brass button next to his name downstairs and he'd buzz me up. Always, I had to knock on the door, which he opened as if I'd come as a mostly pleasant surprise at 2:00 a.m., a minor interruption to his work. He offered me a beer, or a glass of water, or nothing. Then he pounced, direct and disarming, kissed me roughly, removed my clothes and fucked me with the kind of attention and intensity that he brought to his work, an attention that felt inspiring, even infectious. Karim welcomed my enthusiasm but didn't consider it necessary. Afterward, to keep me from dozing off, I think, he would feed me cold pasta puttanesca from a Ball jar, or some take-out falafels wrapped in silver paper. He'd stand, leaning against the loft bed in his kitchen, and watch me eat. Then he'd walk me to the street and hail a cab. He'd try to press a five-dollar bill into my hand—not that this would cover the thirty or forty blocks to my apartment. "Don't be ridiculous," I told him, waving the bill away, climbing into the taxi. I was a feminist.

Once, when I arrived, he met me in the lobby, and we took the elevator together to the floor beneath his, where he showed me a terrible thing—his downstairs neighbor, a sculptor, crushed by a beam from which part of a large-scale wooden sculpture hung. He'd heard the crash, run downstairs, confronted the damage and called 911. He didn't know the sculptor well; she'd moved in only a few months before—but Jesus, but still. The paramedics arrived after Karim had been with her body for over an hour. They asked him a few questions, which he answered. Depressed person? Yes. She had no life, no money, no sex, no enemies and no dealer, just this sculpture, which was so-so, maybe—or maybe it was good. He couldn't say. She drank when she worked, he said. She was drunk now—or had been, before she died. Here was a bottle, here was a glass; they could test her blood alcohol later. The paramedics tried to revive her, but then, without saying much of anything, they moved her body to a gurney and took it away. (A strip of yellow tape stretched across the locked front door, but Karim had a key.)

When he showed me the death scene, I understood how he must feel. He held me tightly, breathed into my neck. I rocked him in my arms; we did it on a quilted mover's cloth on the floor, among broken pieces of sculpture. I had my period, but Karim didn't care, and afterward I found blood on the cloth. Then I noticed blood everywhere; it wasn't even all my blood.

Karim took me upstairs and let me shower and use his towel. When I came out, dressed in my slutty evening clothes, he gave me a blue enamelware bowl of canned chili. Then he walked me up to Houston Street, hailed a taxi and tried to give me five dollars, which I resisted.

It may seem obvious that a relationship like this wasn't going anywhere. I didn't care; I wanted to go everywhere. Karim invited me, twice, to meet his parents, to spend a weekend with his family on Hell's Point, Long Island. It was my first direct experience of architecture—domestic life lived under aesthetic discipline.

THE BRAZIRS' HOUSE in the old summer colony on Hell's Point was defiantly architectural. Every room occupied a different level, and everybody's personal property commingled in a shared dressing room on a mezzanine, whose walls and floor were a blue glass that gave off shadows visible from the living room when you dressed. The house was rigorous and modernist, except for the specially designed item in the dressing room, an altar dedicated to the daily accumulation of clothing and personal effects. The Brazir Tree was (according to the architect, Igor Hermann, who commented on the house in two books, which sat prominently on the Noguchi coffee table in the living room) inspired by the family name, Brazir—actually pronounced *Brajir*. Hermann installed a tree (fabricated, mahogany) at the center of the house, and used its branches as a series of impaling hooks for brassieres and neckties and ticket stubs from Philharmonic concerts. He saw the tree as a kind of metavalet, a sculptural, integrated scrapbook, a changing focal point, a psychic courtyard. Like most architects, Hermann sought to control and direct the gaze. He acknowledged the necessary relationship between the house as a fixed object and the humans who used it—their constant shifting and changing. The house turned inward, rather than outward. It was, for Hermann, a womb—but bright and spare—a blue womb of glass. Natural light poured through clerestory windows into the dressing room, where the Brazir Tree stood silhouetted behind glass, representing nature, or human nature.

Everyone in the house used the Brazir Tree; Hermann's aesthetic discipline prohibited closets or bureaus in the bedrooms. One added a bathing suit or a gauzy dress to the wiry armature of the tree at the end of the day, and plucked one's nightgown off a limb. Mr. Brazir's masculine items dangled among the bras, dandy ties made into a bow, flung shirts from Brooks Brothers worn to a wonderful pulp.

Mrs. Brazir arranged our effects constantly. The picturesque disorder of the tree was a monument to wit, or a witty reference to a monument. You'd find the sleeves of one of his Brooks shirts tied neatly around the waist of Mrs. Brazir's peignoir, gestures like that. Mrs. Brazir's elegance seemed habitual, disciplined, expert. She wore a vial of perfume between her breasts, which she uncorked during the second cocktail of the evening, upended against a finger and daubed into her cleavage.

The perfectly black bathroom Karim and I shared had a red light recessed into the ceiling and a half bathtub sunk into the floor that shot jets of water at your body. To bathe there with the door closed was to go out of this world. (Karim and I soaked all afternoon once, while Mr. and Mrs. Brazir had their adjustments at the chiropractor's.)

The Brazirs dressed up and had cocktails every evening in the living room, where Karim and his mother prevailed upon Mr. Brazir to recite Shakespeare. Or they talked about whether to go see the balanced rock on Sunday or Tuesday. The smallest details mattered. Mornings, we walked down to the beach, a distance of a mile, or sometimes we took bicycles, big lugubrious cruisers that didn't belong to anyone in particular, and went swimming. We didn't just lie in the sand and go splash in the water every hour or so, as my people did. We went specifically to swim, and swam until our arms and legs turned blue. Then we dried off and went home. Intensity was everything to them; they insisted on living intensely in the moment. Sometimes we went to the beach specifically for a picnic, and on those occasions we did not swim. "Let's have champagne and lobster rolls and chocolate cake!" Mrs. Brazir would suggest, then pack and bring these items in minuscule portions. No matter how many of us went on the "picnic," she'd bring one half bottle of champagne, one lobster roll (and a plastic knife) and one piece of cake. In this way, the Brazirs shared the burden of a guest. This seemed like an essential lesson—to live eloquently, yet economically.

Mr. Brazir spoke about rebuilding a car, an Alfa Romeo they'd gotten for nothing. (Far from poor, they lacked only ready money.) One wall of the house opened up by means of hinges, and Mr. Brazir had at some point rolled the car inside. We always had cocktails around the car, and the elder Brazirs sometimes had cocktails in the car—a two-seater, of course—while Karim and I lay on the rug like strewn victims. Or if Mrs. Brazir had had too much to drink the night before, she might remain in bed all day and Mr. Brazir would bring her glasses of ginger ale, and explain, "Mummy's hung." The particular quality of their air held not the tense, angry caesura you feel in some houses, but a loving silence, like a glow coming out of their bedroom, where she lay, I assumed, in a white gown. (She almost always wore white, like a bride.) Only Mr. Brazir penetrated, bearing glasses of ginger ale. I never heard their voices during this exchange, as he pressed the glass into her hand, or set it down on the nightstand beside her; I never heard her say thank you, or him ask if she would like an aspirin. Nothing banal ever happened. The rooms swallowed you in silence, and as you sat in one room, you could not hear voices from the other rooms, or so I thought at first. One afternoon, Karim and I sat in the living room with the Alfa Romeo, which was never really worked on—never a hint of tools, grease or gasoline—only extraordinary, useless and admired. Mr. Brazir had disappeared into the bedroom with a glass of ginger ale. I lay on the rug reading *'Tis Pity She's a Whore* in shameless hope that I could join the conversation over cocktails (though it turned out that the incest conversation happened only one time; the subject moved from theme to theme, and preparation proved impossible). Suddenly I heard ice cubes knocking together as she drank. The sound broke the silence like an avalanche; I realized that the Brazirs communicated to each other without words.

I don't know what they did not talk about—money, ambitions, disappointments. Late in the afternoon, Mrs. Brazir found Karim and me still reading. She said, "Let's go swimming and get salt in our hair and then put on white shirts and go eat mussels at Billy Zee's," and we did that. Mr. Brazir took photographs, developed them in the basement and hung them to dry from wooden clothespins fixed to the Brazir Tree. I think Mrs. Brazir saw herself this way, visually, through his lens, or as if their life were a movie she directed every day.

I saw a book of hers on a table—a simple, personal book. It glowed; it vibrated. I picked it up and read it all, and when I left, I took the book with me.

THE SECOND AND LAST TIME I visited Hell's Point, Mr. Brazir was already sick with the illness that would kill him. He seemed to be in a great deal of pain; I think he felt that he had wasted his time. Mrs. Brazir seemed embarrassed by his short temper, by the way the beautiful, silent rooms held the sharp tone of him. They had gotten by all those years gliding on the surface, and the surface was perfect, like Zamboni ice, until it cracked.

After dinner, Karim and I walked to the beach with a flashlight. No one else appeared, so we lay down in the cold sand and did it quickly. I loved the way his white shirt hung and moved with the motion of his body. (The Brazirs were obsessed with white shirts in summer. Mrs. Brazir insisted that "white must be pristine." The shirts were blindingly white and wrinkly. Sublime dishevelment was the virtue of these shirts; something about them transcended that other quality, of being ironed and businesslike.)

Karim and I did not talk much. He was—I realized this later—too cool to talk much. He had the confidence of a wild animal—he never questioned his instincts. He never asked me about the sex, whether I was satisfied by his intense, distracted hammering; we never discussed it at all. We went back to the silent house, undressed around the Brazir Tree. We hung our clothes on the branches of the tree and went to sleep in our separate rooms.

I woke in the night and looked through the delicate skin of windows into the sky (where the moon hung, waxing gibbous and creamy) and thought, They have the moon.

IN SPITE OF his illness, Mr. Brazir caught a fish for our last dinner, my last among them. He caught it himself somewhere, with a hook and line. It was perfectly illegal, he said with satisfaction; he had gotten away with murder. He invited us to look at the silver skin of the fish, which held rainbow colors in its shingles. Nobody had any idea what kind of fish it was. We called it "the fish" and sometimes "Him."

"Do we want Him in lemon and butter?" Mrs. Brazir asked.

Mr. Brazir announced that we would clean the fish at three o'clock. Mrs. Brazir insisted that first she and I must put on dresses and ride bicycles barefoot to a particular shop to buy lemons. (I wanted to learn everything from her, to inhabit her tone. I still have the stolen book, with entries in her elegant, playful hand: "A beautiful Yale man drinking gin at Thanksgiving. I wanted that one.")

When we returned, Mr. Brazir had found a bottle of champagne in the cellar—something very old, a Taittinger with the label slightly eroded or chewed. He cooked the fish on a tiny hibachi in the garden, and served Him on a platter with His head still on.

He was very small, though. The four of us drank the champagne and shared Him, with slices of lemon. I realized how bourgeois it was to make an evening around quantities of food; better to drink water and eat air.

After dinner, Mr. Brazir rummaged in the pantry— I remember a tea towel tacked up in the door, representing the anniversary of the French Revolution, ten bodies, very well-dressed, severed heads. He returned with his fingers spread around four small lead-colored glasses and a bottle covered with interesting labels. Absinthe was illegal in America, he told us, which I knew from reading postwar novels—it was for information like this that I'd minored in literature. He poured some into each of the glasses and then added water. The absinthe turned milky, though the color of the glasses obscured the full effect.

The drink tasted of licorice and childhood, but quickly went deeper. I began to feel universal and human. The Brazirs understood the discipline of surface—the depth that was protected by surface. The surface functioned as the depth. We were all part of it. What could we do but transcend ordinary, sloppy suffering, rise above it, refuse? I tried to say these things to the Brazirs; it felt like a gift I could offer, to see them in their beauty.

Mr. Brazir began to laugh. His chin fell down on his

chest and he laughed into the soft open collar of his ancient and immaculate white shirt.

Our dirty dinner plates shimmered violently on the tablecloth and the room turned gray-green. Mrs. Brazir uncorked the vial of perfume she wore around her neck and held the opening against one finger. She looked at her finger and said, "Please don't touch anything." Mr. Brazir never stopped laughing.

Karim and I left them there and went for a walk to the beach in the dark. The sand where I lay felt muddy and damp. He pulled up my skirt and rode my body vigorously, his handsome face straining outward, toward the ocean. Just before he came, he slapped my face, and on the way back to the house he said, "I love you."

The next morning, Mrs. Brazir did not rise, and Mr. Brazir scurried off with a glass of ginger ale for her. They hid out, I guess, until Karim took me away. At the ferry, which reeked of diesel and the exhaust of twenty growling cars lined up to board, he kissed me sloppily with his tongue. When I stood at the rail to wave good-bye, my face was still wet. Later I understood that I'd reached the end of my usefulness, like the charming fish called Him we'd murdered and eaten. Karim might have been licking his plate before handing it to a waiter.

THE SNAKE

*D*r. Drema moved twenty-five times before she turned forty-eight. She felt like a different person whenever she lived somewhere new. In all, she'd had consulting rooms in thirteen different cities in the United States and in San Miguel de Allende, Mexico.

It was always sad to shuck an old self. But Dr. Drema grew spiritually from shucking. She gained freshness and vitality, like a snake sliding out of its old skin. *Shpilkes,* her mother called it—ants in the pants. Moving so often had left Dr. Drema's material life in disarray. She kept storage units in several cities on the East and West coasts of the United States (as well as a small house in San Miguel de Allende, which she owned outright), for indispensable articles that she could no longer visualize or name. Someday, when she became less busy, she would sort through these articles or let them go. In the meantime, she paid rents on her storage units, but paid them only after receiving final notice that her possessions would be sold or thrown away. Paying rents late was Dr. Drema's acknowledgment of how conflicted she was about holding on to her past identities. Wouldn't it be better simply to graze across the unspoiled range of one life, like a Neolithic buffalo?

Dr. Drema had no trouble attracting new, necessary patients. For those who remained loyal—those really lost at sea—she held appointments by telephone. In any large or even medium-size city in the western hemisphere, hundreds, thousands of people—and their adolescent children—suffer from anxiety, depression, compulsions, addictions. Such people found Dr. Drema personable, brilliant and charismatic. She belonged to all the important professional organizations. Like buffalo on the range, she roamed free.

SHE'D SEIZED the occasion of her forty-eighth birthday to reinvent herself. On a whim, at a bargain price and with an exceptional interest rate, she moved into the old Customs House in a small New England town at the confluence of a river and an ocean, took a young lover and shaved off eight years. An unpleasant period had just passed, which she wanted expunged from her record—the failed relationship, the car accident, the gallbladder, the chronic fatigue. What had happened to the part of life when every year marked an improving, a flowering out? She gazed through her new salt-speckled windows and said the number forty in her head over and over until it became *her* number—in the same way that she associated candles with the number eight and Tuesdays with the color blue. *Forty, forty, forty.* She said the number until she became the thing. The lie lay near the very core of her identity and intensified ordinary transactions—filling out forms, listening to patients, talking to strangers.

DR. DREMA'S CUSTOMS HOUSE overlooked the estuary of the Glass River. The town itself was formerly working-class and almost defiantly second-rate. Its converted industrial properties drew the sort of young professional people who raised children and confronted primal dramas—or shucked their primal dramas and sent Dr. Drema their bruised adolescent fruits.

The consulting room occupied the second story. Persian rugs covered the floors as well as a couch and a table. More rugs hung from the walls. A tang of history clung to the rugs: old dust, mothballs, something sour underneath the wool that Dr. Drema associated—pleasantly—with the dead. (She had bought the rugs all together at an estate sale when she moved.) Because of the rugs, the consulting room absorbed most of the sounds made there, and the air sparkled with dust. She quickly lost three patients who suffered from allergies. But because demand for her hours exceeded her supply, Dr. Drema could afford to let them go.

She'd come to the small town in pursuit of a dancer called Peter Dvorjak, whom she had met when he performed in a festival in San Miguel de Allende: He begged her to become involved with him. She had been moved by his physicality, by his ability to communicate, through dance, complex psychological states. Peter Dvorjak was drawn, in turn, by Dr. Drema's intensity, intuition, experience and apparent lack of interest in producing a child of her own.

Peter had a child from a previous marriage, a boy called Mikhail, who preferred to be called Mike. Mike was another reason why Dr. Drema became interested in Peter—and why she kept a corn snake in a terrarium in her consulting room, on a table covered with a Persian rug. The snake represented Dr. Drema's commitment to Mike. It also caused the first frisson between herself and Peter, who proved squeamish around thawed mice. Dr. Drema responded generously—generosity was easy—and said the snake could live at her place. She kept the tank in her consulting room, the heart of her house; she didn't mind. Dr. Drema's chief interest in life lay in the study of symbols—and what animal is more symbolic than a snake?

She and Mike named the snake Herpatia. Sometimes, between appointments, Dr. Drema removed Herpatia from the tank and let the snake slither between her hands and around her shoulders. Herpatia's skin felt like fine leather; she was also playful and strong, even *headstrong,* since this quality expressed itself most strongly in her head. One time, Herpatia slithered down the cleavage of Dr. Drema's sweater and emerged above the metal button on her jeans. She made a light, dry sound, traveling, and produced an extraordinary sensation; Dr. Drema had never felt anything like it.

Always, after she had handled the snake, Dr. Drema

washed her hands. Someone at the pet store had said, "You must always wash your hands after handling the snake," plus one other indelible word: *ectoparasite.* Convincing!

Herpatia, in her twenty-gallon tank, became a point of focus for Dr. Drema's patients—a live animal, a mythic presence, but not active enough to distract from the analytic work. The snake also drew Mike naturally into this room of confidences in which anything could be said. Dr. Drema herself found the atmosphere—the live animal, the heavy silence, the glittering bands of dust from old rugs in the air—vicariously liberating. She liked all animals, but especially nonmammals. Before the corn snake—in San Miguel—she used to keep a little yellow bird, which sometimes sat upon her shoulder while she listened to her patients talk.

Sometimes she sat in the consulting room with Mike and kept him company while he handled Herpatia. In Dr. Drema's professional opinion, Mike, at ten, was a too-busy child, always studying Greek or Latin, or tennis, or openings in chess, or practicing Wholfheart on the violin. Peter Dvorjak took his responsibilities as a parent seriously. A serious person himself, he rose every morning at 5:00 a.m. to stretch and do his movement exercises. He then spent hours every day rehearsing—living in his body.

The level of the Dvorjaks' activity intrigued Dr. Drema. Most days, she sat in her consulting room drinking mugs of weak tea, which she replenished with water from her electric kettle, while patients came to her, or called, at their own expense, on the telephone.

Although anguished young professionals were her bread and butter, Dr. Drema found most satisfaction working with adolescents. Their relative openness did not draw her, because the open kind of child did not visit Dr. Drema. The children Dr. Drema saw had clouded over. Their eyes had a milky bluish cast, like Herpatia's eyes before she shed her skin. Some had damaged their surfaces—cut them, or stuffed or shrunk them. Some had no surface at all, only depths, which Dr. Drema tried to plumb in a series of fifty-minute hours. She always had a beautiful career; she intended to write a book on adolescence, the cliff over which one had to persuade oneself to jump. In her dreams she heard the tone she needed; the whole scope of her work revealed itself. But when she woke, she could not hold on to it—sometimes in her dreams this tone was a scent, something wild and animal, and she, Dr. Drema, lay concealed, ready to strike and seize it.

Dr. Drema's large house easily embraced Peter and Mike; she'd planned from the start to take them in. Her income, supplemented by the pittance Peter Dvorjak brought in from his grants, could support them all. Such generosity came easily to Dr. Drema, because Peter brought riches of his own: an energy that came from performing, from creating something original—dances, choreography, and the child.

Dr. Drema and Peter did not understand money in the same way. Dr. Drema maintained a practical relation to the stuff. Money equaled time, energy, power. Peter, on the other hand, claimed not to care. He lived from grant to grant and by teaching. He lived dependently already, as Dr. Drema saw it. And yet he had a charming, stubborn pride, or perhaps just reluctance, when it came to moving permanently into the Customs House. Dr. Drema encouraged Peter to talk about his reluctance so that he might learn to understand and even overcome it.

One morning, Dr. Drema sat at her kitchen table, sipping tea and watching Mike spread honey on a slice of toast. It pleased her to see the child calmly using the things—the knife, the jar of honey, the toast, the plate—that she had bought for their work (she meant their life!) together. Mike dipped the knife into the honey, and a few crumbs migrated into the jar. For Dr. Drema, in some respects a fastidious person, this seemed like a defining moment, though what it defined, she couldn't say. Patients generally loved her for her good qualities: her loud, authentic, life-loving laugh, her irreverence, the depth of her understanding and her empathy with the psychic life of others. She was brilliant but not pretentious; she was down-to-earth; her credentials were impeccable and enviable and might have worked against her were it not for the muddle of her actual life, the charming gap between professional and personal practice. Perhaps because of her profession, people assumed that generosity dominated her character.

The image of crumbs in the honey jar filled Dr. Drema with warmth and longing, sensations followed, as time went by, by a more irritable hunger.

* * *

PETER DVORJAK'S RELATION to his dance company was parental. He ran them; he bullied them. He fretted over his dancers' welfare more than his own, or Mike's. He was also very like them. The company survived on grants, which Peter Dvorjak wrote the way coal miners go down into the mines. He descended into the writing and emerged hours later, the muscles in his arms shiny, his hair standing up on end, his eyes ringed with gray. All his work depended on these peanuts. Sometimes he used Dr. Drema's consulting room, spending hours on his laptop computer, writing a grant for a new piece to be performed in the spring. Dr. Drema encouraged him; a night like this was heaven, as far as she was concerned. She made corn fritters for Mike and herself and served them under a blanket of maple syrup. Sometimes they let Herpatia bask on a pizza stone in a slightly warmed oven while they drank tea at the kitchen table and played Battleship or chess. Upstairs, Peter Dvorjak tapped at his keyboard, used his lighter and wound open the casement before he leaned out of the window to smoke. For Dr. Drema, a large source of happiness consisted of creating conditions that allowed others to work, to behave in a higher way. She did not, herself, have this kind of energy or drive. She hoped to write a book about primal dramas in adolescence; it seemed like work she could do in a slow, solitary way, even in bed, if she wanted to. When she realized that she might be able to wake at eight and lie in bed writing all morning in a notebook, Dr. Drema felt a fresh burst of confidence: She could do this.

She bought a notebook and spent time between her sessions in a state of inspiration. But her notes lost their pungency as they lay dormant. Later, her observations seemed banal, her handwriting indecipherable or unattractive. It was as if the writing had given over its crucial function—to communicate words to herself—and become simply an artifact, a repository of thought. The notebook itself (handsome, leather) seemed more valuable than the words it contained. Eventually, the notebook slipped behind the headboard of Dr. Drema's bed, swallowed as if into her unconscious mind, along with the Moncrieff translation of *The Guermantes Way*, an important pair of glasses, a slender digital camera with photographs of Peter Dvorjak in San Miguel de Allende embedded on a chip inside, a slice of whole grain toast, and a postcard from Dr. Drema's mother, showing the scenic overlook from which, according to Mrs. Drema's note on the back, a man from Idaho had recently pushed his second wife. The notebook slipped behind the headboard and became another artifact of Dr. Drema's psychic life. She stopped thinking about it; she forgot what she had written.

THE TINY THEATER FILLED UP for the first performance of Peter Dvorjak's new show; some in the audience sat on cracks between the seats. Dr. Drema felt surprised that anyone tolerated the shortage without complaining; she was used to getting what she paid for. She'd taken precautions, arrived early, and nabbed a single seat in the front row.

A couple of men climbed over her knees. One man asked the other, "Is this the choreographer you said is sublime, or does he work from a rigid computer-generated formula?"

"Remind me what *sublime* means. Spontaneous?"

"It means awesome."

Before the show began, stagehands emerged from the rear of the theater and laid staging across the corridor that led to the fire exit. It was as if Dr. Drema's body sprouted a hundred buttons that someone simultaneously pushed. The sensation of anxiety approached ecstasy simply because it was so intense. Had she created a too-rigid formula for her psyche, wondered Dr. Drema, digging and probing all day so that her patients, as Freud suggested, could learn to be simply unhappy, in ordinary ways? Had she missed the noisy camaraderie, the heady dangers of real life?

The lights came up. Peter Dvorjak knelt over a suitcase. Dr. Drema relaxed immediately; she understood symbols, baggage. He'd covered his powerful, toned body in loose clothing—work pants and a work shirt in martial green. Peter Dvorjak spoke of a lover, clearly male, who had "gone in" when he was twenty-three. The story immediately drew her in, and Dr. Drema forgot about the discomfort of the too-few seats. Apart from the threat of fire, she felt happy; she loved to listen. Listening was her calling, attention without action, noticing what part of the story was being withheld. She had less sensitivity to movement, though she liked to watch.

Peter Dvorjak moved fluidly across the stage, commu-

nicating in supple or intentionally awkward gestures something human that transcended analysis. Dr. Drema watched,
impressed, slightly outside the moment. She enjoyed being
part of a full house, watching her young lover move across
the stage, curl up into a plastic cube, roll ecstatically across
the floor, rise and grind and tango with the imaginary prisoner and move as if he were making love to this other man,
although it wasn't sex: It was tango, hip-hop and ballet.
Dr. Drema's skin pricked up. She felt a chill, in spite of the
body-heated air.

A woman appeared on the stage and began to sing a haunt-
ing melody. The company joined her, dancers of various colors, mostly androgynes, very slight. Peter Dvorjak looked
like an Amazon, except that he was short, his tragedy—or
maybe the source of his machismo—as a dancer. The dancers whirled across the stage into one another's arms. The
smallest ones lifted and tossed the heaviest like Hacky Sacks.
Dr. Drema experienced it all intensely. Possibly the glass
of wine she'd had with dinner? She rarely drank, because
of the health risks, and the loss of self-control. Now every
jeté and glissade, all the grands ronds de jambe, planted
her more firmly in her chair. The planted feeling was not
rootedness; it was a sensation of being nailed down in her
role as observer, as *audience.* The situation became almost
immediately unbearable, not because Dr. Drema could not
bear it, but because she wanted to be part of the movement.
She began, almost mischievously, to rub her hands over and
over each other, producing a dry, sandpapery sound. Soon

the audience picked up on her friction and began to rub their hands together, too. Dr. Drema had started it, and now everyone joined in, and Peter Dvorjak improvised, moving to the rhythm and sound of the hands.

"That was weird," someone said at intermission.

"*She* started it," said someone Dr. Drema couldn't see.

Yes, no, thought Dr. Drema. She could argue with equal vigor on one side or the other.

At the reception afterward, Peter introduced her and announced to his dancers, "The doctor and I are lovers." The loose, expanding confederation of dancers and aco-lytes battled with one another to sit next to Dr. Drema on the slippery cushions; they spilled beer on her, offered her cigarettes. They pressed boldly up against her, murmuring, "That's cool," and "That's hot—your being older."

Dr. Drema asked them about the performance, what they thought it meant. The prisoner's crime was not sig-nificant, the dancers agreed, because the play wasn't about guilt or innocence, but about essence, and how the state, in some profound sense, controls the essence of who we are—whether we are "inside" or "outside" the margins of society. A young dancer said, "The prison system is a powerful engine of hegemony; the play's point is that we operate within that system, whether we agree with it or not." Another dancer said, "Really, it's just the story of Peter's first love, his sexual awakening. That's what his work is always about."

*   *   *

THE NEXT MORNING, Dr. Drema walked downtown to a gift shop and bought three pair of fuzzy lobster slippers for Peter Dvorjak, Mike and herself. Dr. Drema thought the lobster slippers might bind the three of them symbolically while also acknowledging the shell that kept each of them protected and private. (Mike was a Cancer and had a hard shell.) She hoped Mike and Peter would think of her when they wore the slippers.

She was walking home when her cell phone rang—her mother, who called every Saturday. Mrs. Drema was a vessel for news from the town where Dr. Drema had grown up. Over the course of the week, she filled and then bubbled over with the dramas of her town—the accidents that were not quite accidents, the murders and illnesses. For a town, the numbers were high. There was the man who worked at the boatyard and had encased his ex-wife in fiberglass, the couple in the old apartments behind the Catholic church who drugged tourists and then used them sexually, the man from Idaho who had thrown two consecutive wives from the cliffs into the ocean. Many of these felons or their victims had passed through Mrs. Drema's third-grade class, and Mrs. Drema remembered significant, retrospectively revealing details about each of them. She saw into their reasons and personal histories with compassion and empathy, and Dr. Drema had been profoundly influenced by her mother's methods of analysis.

She listened now out of a complicated sense of duty; talking about the disturbances of strangers was their way of keeping connected and close.

"You feel the murderer is less guilty of his crime because of his violent history," Dr. Drema said when Mrs. Drema went quiet.

"I suppose I do."

After three-quarters of an hour, Dr. Drema let the conversation stall. "Well," she said, "save time next week?"

"Same time, you mean."

"That's what I said," said Dr. Drema pleasantly.

Mrs. Drema would have loved nothing more than to listen to the lives of Dr. Drema's patients, not out of a frivolous curiosity, but from an earnest interest in humanity. Professional ethics, however, compelled Dr. Drema to keep her analysands' stories confidential. And so she continued to do what she had done best all her life—to listen, to withhold.

THAT NIGHT in the Customs House, Dr. Drema slept intensely. She dreamed of the town where she had originated— the town at the root of herself, or, rather, the reservoir underneath the town. Here, on a lake in the dark, she discovered an underground boat, which carried her across the slow black water under no sky, and after she had paddled for a time, she reached a stony island where underground birds made their nests in underground trees covered with pale green lichens. Dr. Drema spread her blanket, unwrapped a meal of bread and cheese and ate, with pleasure, in the company of worms. This rare waterfront property seemed exceedingly valuable and desirable, but also interior, dark and original, like a mind.

Over coffee in the morning, Peter smoked in his mournful Eastern European manner. Dr. Drema knew she would miss him when she moved, this carelessly disheveled young man who looked so beautiful smoking in her kitchen, and begged her for love. She felt shy, in a middle-aged way, about her body, and she'd understood from the beginning the toll such a relationship could take on her energy and time and ultimately her amour propre. In spite of what people said about analysts, she had to be sane: Sanity was the sine qua non of her credibility. Also, Peter had his habits of movement, and she had hers. Already she felt the mobilizing signs: an itchiness like the beginning of a cold; her *shpilkes*.

SOME OPPORTUNITY PRESENTED itself in California; Dr. Drema sold the Customs House and moved. She gave Peter one of the Persian rugs he'd admired, and put the rest in storage; she offered Herpatia and the tank, as well. Mike registered sadness, even a little wild grief at the loss of Dr. Drema, who promised that they could keep in touch by telephone. He wore almost compulsively the pair of lobster slippers she'd given him. Peter agreed to keep the snake under conditions that Mike tried to meet. He never forgot to feed Herpatia her frozen pinkies until summer, when he went away to a camp devoted to violin instruction and Jewish spirituality.

By this time, Peter had become interested in the snake, the way it moved and settled and used its body. He liked the way Mike and Herpatia interacted, the dry sound Herpatia made when she slid across Mike's loosely open hands or wound around his shoulders. He hoped soon to feel comfortable handling the snake himself; he planned to do some choreography around the idea of a man learning to trust a snake.

One morning, in the spirit of a gift, Peter released a live rat into the tank. He'd bought the rat because he wanted Herpatia to experience authentically the drama of the hunt, the intensity of nature. He lit a cigarette and stood before the primal stage: a twenty-gallon tank in which the hunter faces her prey and the prey confronts his destiny. He watched as Herpatia ignored and then approached the rat with her head. She struck almost diffidently, and then appeared to wait. Peter had already choreographed the sequence of events in his mind: the heightening effects of the hunt, the necessary idea of fear, the prey representing itself as an appetizing vibration.

When he saw the determined yellow incisors tearing into the flesh and the spastic movements of the sinuous body, he swore at the rat and shouted meaningless words to the snake. His cigarette dropped from his lips into the tank and fumed around the scene like dry ice. Peter wrapped his arms around the tank and lifted, as if it would help, in spite of the impediments of the reptile heater and its electrical cord, to move the primal stage elsewhere.

AMOR AND PSYCHO

I. Psycho

Psycho wrote in the morning—a rant about giving some bald guy head in the bathroom of the gas station at dawn, something she hadn't actually done lately—then she walked into the park and paced the playground for an hour, riffing. Hyperarticulate self-revelation was Psycho's talent. She illuminated experiences other people would avoid, repress or hide. Poetry was a blood sport in our foggy little town, attracting dropouts and misfits, theater freaks hungry for a solo, and a few of the angry college-bound. Twice a year, poets faced off in the meeting hall of the Caballeros de Colombo, and the top scorer got a chance—a chance no one had ever taken—to unravel her shitty life at the Grand Slam Finals in San Francisco at the Warfield.

Freestyling was how Psycho elevated her consciousness.

Our whole team aspired to this condition, but Psycho had the most confidence in our dumbfuck lives as material. She came out to her mother, for example, at a slam. Psycho wasn't actually gay; she was bi; she was whatever. She came out at every slam; she came out, really of her own mouth, kissing Heather in front of Boz Blacks's Store, where ten-year-olds bought cigarettes—but everything she said was true, or became retroactively inevitable. Psycho was the first girl I ever heard use the word "incested" as a verb. This turned out to be the least original thing about her. "When I speak my shit," she said, "I want you to see the beautiful ugliness of the world, like a cathedral made of tin foil gum wrappers, dead cigarettes, condoms and bright-colored suckers."

WE WATCHED in awe during Harald Bugman's memorial service at the Odd Fellows Hall as Psycho killed it:

> My teeth chatter at death like pecked letters. Read them
> in the fog at dawn / down by the river that runs under
> the concrete bridge / where someone has painted in urgent
> red / writing: Harald Bugman was here.

On that terrible occasion we trusted Psycho to shine a light on the darkness; hers was the voice we most needed. We'd already heard a loose cannon, Jane Jones, go off about some cousin of hers who had committed suicide while taking meds for anxiety and acne. As if this had anything to do with Harald, as if the point of the story was the overmedication of the mentally ill in America. Jane droned on about how parapsychotic schizophrenia was a disease registered in the DSM, an amazing book; the library should get a copy of the fourth edition so the whole town could benefit from this diagnostic tool, used constantly by all mental-health professionals. Harald's mother, Babe Bugman, looked, at this point, literally breakable, practically shattered already. While nobody expected the memorial to turn into a celebration of Harald's life, exactly—his death at nineteen was tragic, stupid—it shouldn't turn, either, into a recitation of everybody's story about their mentally ill relatives and the pharmaceutical-industrial complex.

Then Psycho stood up, creating a frisson of expectation: Now any drama could be narrated. She spoke intimately to everyone at the same time and burned with a secret energy. Her voice seemed to come from a deep place, like a funnel or a sinkhole.

Harald Bugman *had* made a permanent mark, like blood or hazardous waste, a wild scribble that lived. The very name—Harald—in Psycho's mouth made everyone proud, made everyone weirdly hungry. In the magic way of memorials, three trestle tables in the hall filled up with free-range meatballs, logs of fresh goat cheese and homemade bread, and salads of baby lettuce with bright orange nasturtium petals and blue borage flowers out of which earwigs and small spiders crawled. Pat Estevez made pupusas to order on her little hot plate; somebody roasted a pig out back, and the locavores formed an important knot around the fire to discuss its provenance. The beer, wine, weed and apple pies were locally sourced; our town began to love itself again. The only flaw: Harald was dead and his mother, Babe Bugman, looked startled and destroyed, her visage ravaged. Her visage ravaged, her ravaged visage! No matter the level of suffering, Psycho turned everything into language. She couldn't help herself; she was a bard. Besides eating and drinking and Psycho, there was so little (Babe Bugman's ravaged visage and the bizarre RC wall hangings belonging to the Odd Fellows with their occult symbolism and vividly bleeding hearts) to make Harald's death real. Because Harald had died violently, there was no body to focus on, no coffin, and, for the immediate family at least, no God.

ALL PSYCHO ASKED FOR was the chance to stare freely, and free-associate. Olivia's striped hat, Amit's nose ring, the wings of Heroine's blue eye shadow, Roy's admirable eyebrow and the star tattooed behind her left ear. She wanted to remember the last pure time she wore sneakers, lace-up ones. White Keds, with a blue line around the rubber.

It happened freshman year—that she became Psycho. Before, she was just Psyche—a given, hippie name. In the eighth grade, the magic powers of witchy girls came on like ecstasy, filled us up like fresh air, except it wasn't fresh. It was old. All the girls hated on Psyche because she was fairly sexually advanced, so everybody called her a ho and said she was a hellaslut. Psyche went into the den of girls; down by the taqueria they pulled each other's hair.

She came out the other side re-created as Psycho. No one could get to her then, except Harald. No one but him was more whacked and brilliant than her.

WHEN SHE FREESTYLED, Psycho just stood there spouting out of some necessary instinct, changing the words around so they sounded right but didn't quite make sense, or said something she hadn't known before: *Glowering noun* or *souring gown* or *flowering town.*

> *How can I trust you or*
> *organized pustule*
> *Blown man or wingspan or*
> *spring ham*

> *If you can't escape*
> *Create chaos.*

> *My frontal cortex. It's a city I built with cardboard and the*
> *X-Acto knife my boyfriend Harald used to cut his wrists.*

And then, famously, Harald cut his wrists, enhancing her reputation. But Psycho remained humble.

*Words appeared like reverse graffiti, bleached and burned
onto the dirty canvas of my mind—spilled, bleeding. My
voice is not me. It's a stick in a desert, writing in dirt.*

After Harald, then after Heather, Psycho's next lover was
a man named Mr. Avery, very adult, very skilled, she said.
He was a total secret—forty-two, forty-five—and lived two
towns away with his wife. We laughed too loudly when Psycho said "skilled." Sex still made us nervous. Not that we
minded sexual talk, sexual jokes, sexual innuendo, sexual
confidences—and like anybody else we released sexual ten-
sion by laughing.

In the afternoons, Psycho sat on the big wooden bench
on the cliff overlooking the beach like the nymph Psyche on
her rock or crag, waiting for her mythical lover, Amor. Psycho sat there waiting for Mr. Avery. Only she wasn't waiting.
She was *writing*. We could see her lips move.

Every year, a cliff crumbled, carrying someone down;
young lovers were particularly vulnerable. One day, Mr.
Avery didn't come, and Psycho turned his tragic drama into
the stuff she turned everything into.

*Even though the Averys' baby was born dead, Mrs. Avery
insisted the baby was* still *born. If you're still long enough,
we could accuse you of being* still still, *a redundant
condition like life itself. Imagine all the bores who have
still been born.*

In preparation for the Grand Slam Finals, Psycho went downtown to the bathroom at the gas station—the headquarters of her early bold gestures—and cut off all her hair. Then at the throwdown on Saturday night, she rapped about her hair—pretty, pretty hair—she wanted it gone, and now it was. Beauty was ugly, et cetera. She did a freestyle called "My Mom Looks Like Hell—in a Good Way." It was just Psycho up onstage, basically bald, rocking it, and her mom in the blackened theater, taking it:

Sometimes Mom looked like a wind-wrecked face / at the front of a ship, a mythic beast / or made of snakes, her face a mess of ess / -shaped lines, or came covered in mud, green and cracked / Sunglasses on the whole year she fucked Stan / O, black-eyed beauty! / Stirred her drink with a finger and sucked it off / Once she saw what she'd done to that deer she backed up the car and hit it again.

Psycho's mom left the throwdown that afternoon—or maybe it was another afternoon; Psycho adjusted facts for realistic effect—and drove into a baby, a three-year-old, at a crosswalk. It could have been the lithium, and—face it—a helpless baby shouldn't be out on the street on its own at dusk. Still. Psycho told the truth before it happened. Her mom flattened like a cartoon character, as if she'd run over herself.

Empathy isn't real. It's chemical, like endorphins when
you run. When I stopped touching my mother, her
empathy dried up. Now she has emotional eczema. This
year she hit a baby with her car. Now she takes even more
medication. The baby will live; it's a miracle baby. Even
now, it's suing her ass.

Psycho's enemies complained to the school board: "Girls who talk dirty and dress skanky shouldn't be allowed to work with kids." But Psycho loved her community service, teaching fourth graders to speak up and shout out. She taught them spoken word, hip-hop. Corrupting youth was the best and purest thing in her life, she said. She loved their innocence, their depravity, their potential. She pushed her students to dig deeper than they thought they wanted to; she made them sound stranger and more interesting than they were.

AS A JOKE, Psycho went out for baseball. Those girls like Greek heroes, ropy legs and broad shoulders, their attitudes of power as they held their iPods and baseball bats—Psycho became one of them. This happened in the spring, before Harald died, the season of the new rope swing going up at the swimming hole, the season of strapless prom dresses, high heels, asparagus and apricots. Softball took her—to Wineland Valley, Strawberryville—even Hawk Park and River City. After Maria Cabeza went down with her pregnancy, Psycho became the pitcher. She pitched like she free-styled, taking a stance, throwing herself out there. She took the title at the County-Wide Throwdown with a freestyle on the dual nature of balls so mesmerizing, no one remembered two words of it the minute it was over.

Psycho's dad couldn't watch her play, or help with driving. Her mom drove to every game, a hundred miles down the 28, or the 116, or the 1.

PSYCHO MADE THE CUT—we knew she would—for the Grand Slam Finals at the Warfield. Our team went in the van to watch. Psycho's mom drove; she had a new paper license. Even Psycho's dad came. First we waited in a line halfway down Market Street, where a bunch of thugs tried halfheartedly to threaten us. Then we were in, up in the second balcony. The lights went down, and the grand master pumped the crowd. A chica read a poem in Spanish, her voice riding like a Lexus over the awkward tangle of vowels and consonants, and it sounded so fluent—how could she speak so quickly?—and so wise. Then she translated the poem and it was the same old bullshit they feed all the Catholic girls: Love is everything, love fills the soul, love is our highest purpose, life pales and I am nothing without love.

Next came a poet with a big red flower in her ear, and a case number—#389214B—written across her T-shirt in Sharpie. She riffed about how she was going to be released from the welfare system the day she turned eighteen. She had sixty-five days left of high school, plans for college. But without her group home, she'd be homeless. Her caseworker said that if she dropped out of school or got pregnant, she'd qualify for help. "You think I should get pregnant?" "I'm just giving you the information." Then came a dude whose family came from the hills of China, via Laos, Vietnam and Thailand to Oakland. *What are you?* people asked. *What are you? What are you?*

"Marry me," someone screamed from the floor.

Somebody said, "Where's Psycho?" And then there she was, onstage for the first round, and our team went crazy. We went crazy screaming her name until the whole Warfield went quiet, waiting.

IN THE STORY of Amor and Psyche, the young maid is cursed, through no fault of her own. Her parents, obedient to fate, set their daughter out in the elements upon a rock crag to be ravished and used. Psyche waits. A black hole surrounds her, the sky darkens, a wind kicks up, and she is blown upward and wafted into the valley below. Amor, whose job it is to transport the vulnerable and valuable virgin into the hoariest arms possible, instead takes Psyche for himself, not revealing his true identity. Psyche, who has been led to expect a miserable and oppressed existence, feels slightly relieved, sexually; her lover is sweet-smelling, soft-skinned and reasonably tender; her situation could be worse. In this way, she begins to understand the possibility of desire. And yet she can't see her lover; the condition of her marginal happiness is total ignorance. And, really, how long can that last?

Those girls were like the dumb sheep who lived next to the garage. / The lamb down with her elbows in the mud / sucking on her mother's tits while the big sheep peed upon her head. / The girls at school said they were glad there was no more boy-on-girl sex / only natural interaction between beings. / They were, it turned out, the majorettes of the future / dressed up, bold-faced with boiled teeth / and padded bras, carrying sticks.

After Psycho, more poets came on. They spat rhymes about police brutality and street violence, about nickel nines and Wendy's parking lot, about Oscar Grant III being shot in the back on a BART train by the Oakland police while lying facedown, unarmed. The gesture—arms floating up and down like birds' wings, the back crumpling inward—kept returning in poems about the streets, as if it were the universal gesture of innocence. Kids troped toward and veered from suicide. Palestine and the effects of white phosphorous shimmered in the foreground, and a Sikh kid forced the audience to point at him and shout out "Sick! Sick!" to duplicate the judgment that rained down every day on the turban he couldn't wear to school. We listened, our mouths hanging open. The Warfield filled with the popping sound of silence breaking. Psycho's two estranged parents sat vibrating together in the second balcony, but Psycho didn't come back for the second round. She didn't even place.

II. Georgie

Georgie looked in the mirror and realized that without hair she had no face. She had only a head, a globe turning on the axis of her neck. Eyes, mouth, nose—but no face. Her face was history.

She looked gorgeous and irresistible without hair, her new boyfriend, Ralph, said wildly. She looked so intense and theatrical, he could no longer bear to sleep with her. He said he felt weak, cowardly and defective. Georgie agreed.

Ralph's mother sent her a reusable barf bag. Georgie had never even met Ralph's mother—but they were sisters in cancer! The barf bag, like all the other accoutrements of this disease, came in pink. A joke that was not a joke, like all jokes. A barf bag! Mouth spray! A toothbrush! What more thoughtful gifts could you give somebody getting chemotherapy?

What Georgie wanted, really, was sex—vigorous human sex with a reasonable person, preferably of the other gender. When she divorced, several women she knew called with offers. She said she would think about it—and she did think about it. Who wouldn't?

*   *   *

THE BAD NEWS STARTED on election night. Georgie had some friends over, and they ate lamb and drank cold rosé from Spain and watched on television as the evening went as badly as possible for their side. Their candidate lacked charisma, but they had tried to believe in him. After the results came in, they read their fortunes on Georgie's Chinese sticks, and Georgie's said something like "You will know illness before old age."

"No fair," her friend Babe said. "I took two. I took yours."

This was true—greedy Babe.

"It doesn't matter," Georgie said.

"Take another."

Georgie's second fortune read: "What you ask for is unreasonable and you will not get your wish."

BEFORE HER FIRST CHEMO, everyone said Georgie was lucky to have had experience with psychotropic drugs, because nuclear medicine tripped you out. It *was* trippy, and afterward she felt poisoned, as advertised; the Popsicle red medicine turned her pee red. She spent the night in a little hotel just a few blocks from the Cancer Center. In the morning, she tried to give the doorman three dollars for carrying her bag. He pulled his hand back from hers as if she were on fire or poisonous and said, "No, no, no!"

Georgie's first night home, Babe came over to shear her hair. It would fall out anyway, so why not? They dragged two lounge chairs out onto the lawn and watched the sunset over the ocean as Babe cut the hair down to the stubble of all the colors Georgie had dyed it over the years, a kaleidoscope of color embedded in her follicles. (Her features were still strong, though, Babe said, and her eyes glowed like bonfires.) Georgie realized that what she thought of as "my face" and "my self" enclosed just a small part of something larger. The face was a few planes of flesh stretched over a structure of bones—frontal, temporal, parietal, occipital. Georgie knew this from looking at skeletons; she was a kind of skeleton herself, her body a loose confederation of bones held together by joints and a temporary binding of muscles, enclosed by a skin that marked the boundary between herself and everything not herself. The profound moment of confronting her hairless head made Georgie want to have sex immediately. Dr. Daly had promised the drugs would send her into a fierce and irrevocable menopause; this could be her last egg drop. Lying on her back in the lounge chair and looking up at the sky, she felt like someone waiting to be hit by a train. She watched the sun burn on the horizon before it fell through a hole in the ocean.

A whippoorwill sang. Babe held Georgie's hand. They drank tea as the moon rose yellow and full, a hunting moon. Owls flew through the air like thrown bricks.

"I feel like a werewolf," Georgie said, "only my hair falls out instead of growing in."

They slept outside, under heavy woolen blankets. In the morning, when Georgie got up to make coffee, she saw the moon still hanging above the ocean, as if someone had forgotten to put it away.

HER PUBIC HAIR fell out. Funny, because she'd had bikini waxes for years, and associated pubic hair with the triumphant face of her Russian aesthetician in San Francisco holding up the terrible strips of fabric. Her ex-boyfriend, Ralph, preferred his women "with," as he put it. Maybe he didn't say "my women." But he did say "with," as if there were only two kinds of women in the world. (Now she shattered the binary with her clumps and bald spots!) Ralph dumped her when she told him what she had, when she first found out. He hugged her; he patted her back and said he wished he could "be there" for her. But he hardly knew her at all.

Her hair fell out; fruit flies emerged. At first, they seemed concentrated around some bananas she kept in a bowl. But then one day she found a feathery cluster of them in the hair by her ear as she read *Illness as Metaphor*. Was she the fruit they wanted?

GEORGIE FOUND a new lover without too much trouble. The two of them carried on a torrid correspondence by e-mail during the break that followed her last chemotherapy. His profile on the Internet drew her because he wore a black watch cap; she'd also worn a black watch cap since her chemo started and the hair on her head fell out, as well as all the rest of her hair, including her eyelashes and eyebrows.

His screen name: T-Bone. He asked her to call him T.

He wrote in a sensitive way that accepted her as she was (sick), and then she wrote, raveled out a few selected details and asked about his life. He told her about his two kids and how he'd worked as a full-time stay-at-home dad until they were grown, and Georgie wrote back, telling him how much she'd wanted children, at least one child, but by the time her print shop was established, it was too late, or at least too late to start again, and the marriage came apart anyway, and—well, she and T wrote back and forth, revealing certain details and concealing others. Georgie wasn't exactly new to Internet courtship.

T seemed different. For one thing, he lived in the Midwest—Iowa or Ohio or Nebraska. He offered to fly out to San Francisco on the first day of her radiation to meet her. He didn't have cancer—just the hat. But he seemed drawn to the specific signal, the cancer beam of Georgie's black watch cap. "I want to know you for a long time," he wrote. "But I want to start knowing you now, while you're still in the thick of this. I want to see you now, without hair. I want to hold you this way, as you are when we meet."

In a certain kind of vulnerable moment, this seemed plausible and romantic. T's words made Georgie feel hot and damp all over with a moisture that she felt must be the last of its kind. He wrote that he wanted to make love to her now, bald and nauseated. Even her ex-husband, a generous man, hadn't offered that.

She wrote back to T and asked if he was kidding. He wrote back with a flight number and a time of arrival and the name of a not-bad hotel where he'd made a reservation, and the name of a restaurant near the infusion center where he would meet her for lunch. She brewed herself a pot of tea to steady her nerves, and wrote: "OK!"

IN THE GOWN ROOM, while savagely ripping tags from her expensive new lingerie, Georgie met a young woman named Linette. Linette had come from Irian Jaya, in Indonesia, and also had cancer in her breast—but a different kind. The cancer had grown on the outside of her skin, and also inside her chest cavity and bones, and it had spread, inoperable. Linette said these things in the words she had been given, the simple declarative sentences that announced her fate like a verdict from a judge. Linette asked Georgie what kind of chemo she'd had, and when Georgie told her, she said her doctors wanted her to do that protocol, too, but she was afraid it would make her even sicker than now. What did Georgie think? How sick had the chemo made Georgie? Did she still feel like herself? Georgie said, "Good question"—she no longer knew who she was. Linette said she just wanted more time to be in her body—but she wanted to be herself. "What would you do if you were me?" Linette asked.

Georgie said she didn't know, that she could only say what the chemo made her feel like—both sick and hungry, not necessarily for food. She felt poisoned by the toxic red junk that turned her toenails black, but also stronger than she had ever known herself, more interested in living. If anyone had asked her five years ago what she would think was important if she had cancer, she would have said nutrition, herbs, affirmations, et cetera. But once the disease took up residence in her, she became a tyrannical landlord, relentless in her struggle to evict. Linette stood before Georgie in her thin gown with its complicated ties—so complicated someone had actually posted a diagram in the gown room showing in detail how to weave all the loose strings together—and said, "What would you do if you were me?" Georgie could not even pretend to say. She took tiny Linette in her arms and for the first time in weeks felt her own body as a solid, as a force. She saw herself as one of the lucky ones, almost at this point a fraud. Now holding Linette, her sister, in the gown room, Georgie caught the odor of something deep: the breath of mortality. Linette's thin arms held Georgie fiercely. Georgie could feel (through skin and bone) the quick beating of Linette's heart, like a small bird struggling at a window.

A few minutes later, Georgie dressed and hurried from the building. What a ridiculous schedule she had laid out for herself: radiation, followed by lunch with a stranger, and then, if all went well, sex in T's hotel room. Later, she could, if she wanted, go up Divisadero to her friend Katya's house, where Katya would feed her some delicate broth and a glass of wine. Georgie swore off meat and sugar and liquor after the diagnosis, but when she saw the amount of poison coursing through her body, she relented, or rather protested, and ate and drank small portions of anything that gave her pleasure—roast chicken, a moderate pour of Sancerre, even an organic burrito with a dollop of sour cream.

Cabs circled around Oncology—like hawks, Georgie thought as she stepped into one. She could have walked to the restaurant to meet T, but that was an unrealistic plan if she hoped even to consider sex in the afternoon. Already she felt curled in at the edges. Yet here lay the secret gift of the disease—the heightening, the sharpening. She felt alive; she'd never been so constantly aware of it. After she gave her destination to the driver and settled into the cab, Georgie closed her eyes and concentrated on meeting T, on building appetite.

He didn't disappoint, exactly. Although almost from the first it was clear that although he seemed a good person in every way—not the serial killer creep Katya had warned her about—T was not, under the usual circumstances, her kind of guy. But the usual circumstances had been fed eight doses of tamoxifen and then irradiated. She felt, with this man who had flown from Ohio or Iowa or Nebraska to meet her, a lightness and ease, the oppressive weights of history and the future lifted. In many ways, the disease cured the worst afflictions of this sick capitalist society: It dissipated materialist impulses, lifted the tiny burdens that tied people Gulliver-like to earth and made one more aware of the small hot fire burning inside. T seemed smart enough, attractive enough. They recognized each other immediately; under the black watch caps, they wore the same shadowy bristle.

They drank green tea and ate bowls of fresh fruit, and although Georgie tasted only a little, she felt the vitamins and moisture penetrate her tired cells. Her tissues waxed and swelled, her blood sped up and, yes, her body buzzed!

T also consumed eggs and bacon and home fries and toast—they'd starved him on the plane. Although she had to keep her eyes averted from the food, his hunger roused Georgie's. The fruit in her bowl smelled decadent, alcoholic, and she pushed it to one side while T ate and told her how out of character it was for him to fly across the country to meet a woman—but, yes, he had done it before.

He took her hands across the table and kissed them and looked into her eyes.

"I'm glad you let me come," he said.

Georgie reached out and touched the indentation beneath his right ear. A slight electric charge ran up her arm.

At the hotel, a sudden weakness came over her. In the excitement of meeting T, she had not stopped to wash her hands before she ate. Her hands, her clothes smelled of Linette; she tasted Linette on the end of her tongue. Georgie opened the windows in T's room and let in the city sounds. Suddenly a tear fell out of her eye like a stone and landed on the carpet.

"I'd like to take a bath," she told him, and he went to the closet and pulled out the hotel's leopard-print robe for her to use. She found his razor and his toothbrush and a carefully rolled tube of toothpaste on the sink. A faux-leather ditty bag. All this effort, this human vanity. She had to struggle to be part of it.

In the bath, she pressed the soap to her nose and breathed in. She'd brought her essential oils, and with all the strength in her arm she shook droplets into the water. The familiar aromas of cloves and roses and ylang ylang came up, the smell she thought of as herself.

She reappeared wearing the leopard robe and let it fall. T lay in the bed already, slipped between the sheets like a dinner mint. His ardor was touching; he was almost too gentle. His hand on her breast smelled of Linette, his tongue in her mouth, his fingers inside her. He came inside her, too—why the hell not?

It all went well enough—it went very well. Apart from the smell of death in her nose, Georgie felt light and alive. His body next to hers felt good. He did not go to sleep immediately, but caressed her skin with his palms. Two hours later, though, she was burning up from the inside. She had to call the emergency room doctor, even though she knew the symptoms of infection. She and T dressed and walked to Walgreens at 4:00 a.m. to pick up her prescription; he wrapped a wing of his bulky midwestern coat around her. In the morning, she vomited in the bathroom while he looked at the *New York Times* over free coffee in the lobby. She brushed her teeth with her pink toothbrush; then they took a walk on Ocean Beach before she drove him to the airport.

The wind seemed to sweep the smell from her; she blew her nose bloodily into a tissue and afterward felt better.

At the airport, he insisted that she not park, but leave him at the curb. "Call me anytime," he told her. "Call if you need me—and call if you don't need me." He kissed her on the mouth and smiled into her eyes. Tears brimmed on her eyelids and she made her eyes swallow them down. They drizzled back into her body as she accelerated onto the freeway, a greedy girl who had gotten at least something of what she wanted and was now free to be no one, nothing, not even human, for anyone.

III. Babe

Cutting made Harald feel alive; the more he cut, the more he felt. He didn't have a suicidal fantasy. There was nothing he cared about enough to die for. He knew what love was, probably, although it pained him to think of those afternoons in bed with Psycho, her flat chest rubbing against his as she seemed to be moved and swayed by some blast of erotic agony, her narrow face gouged with pain, her small teeth biting the sheets. He refused to die for love. If Psycho or his mom thought he had died for them, even posthumously it would tarnish him. He did not want to think about Psycho because she reminded him that he had betrayed her by falling in love when they'd agreed that love was bourgeois and stupid, what Psycho's cheerful mother felt when she climbed into bed at night with Psycho's new fat father—love as a last resort, love as gratitude, love as filler. Worse, he had fallen in "love" with someone else—a sous-chef at Café Malatesta. He'd deceived Psycho, even though she never asked him to be faithful; she sneered at the claustrophobic virtue of fidelity and agreed with him about the pointlessness of gender.

He sterilized his X-Acto knife—he wasn't an idiot—and began very high up on his right arm. He made the first cut shallow; the first cut was a test.

He imagined Psycho in the backseat of a car with her little sister, Charity, and her inanely happy mother and her new father, all of them singing feel-good songs in harmony. He wondered whether Psycho, in spite of her Goth / bisexual pretensions, ever got into it. He thought she probably did. (On her first date with her new girlfriend, Psycho asked Harald to come along. That's how insecure she was. Harald sat in the backseat all night and didn't say a word. They drove to the beach and walked on the sand in the dark, Harald following a few steps behind, like a ghost. They drank green chlorophyll drinks with antioxidants to prolong the lives they'd talked at length about throwing away. They smoked weed and made out, and Harald took part as much as Harald ever took part in anything.)

He thought of his own sister, Emma, who was twenty and worked in a toy store, where she was a fucking genius. The two of them used to walk home together after school and bake muffins in a toy oven. He used to get into that, especially if he'd been smoking weed, which he had been. In the morning, after his parents left for work, he used to take a book into their bed and read. His mom had painted the bedroom red and gold—this just before she left his dad, whom everyone called "Bug," short for Bugman, their last name. It was her last big paint job. The bedroom wasn't really even a room, just an attached shed his father and he had caulked the brains out of one Saturday afternoon. The shed didn't have heat—you could see wild mustard and calla lilies and gorse bushes through slivers in the walls—but it had an altar his mother had bought at a flea market in the city and a collection of turquoise Buddhas and those red-gold walls and the warmest down comforter in the house. His mother had a tiny picture of him—of Harald—in a funky gold frame on the nightstand on her side, beside her carafe of water and her amber jar of excellent antidepressants. Harald had cut himself for the first time in his parents' bed. He felt safe there.

Now he wondered, idly, drawing a line parallel to the first line in his upper arm, whether this bed would be his last. A dramatic thought—Psycho would slap him, sit on him, tickle and humiliate him for it. He knew—they both knew—that the only power they had was not to give a shit. Harald *didn't* give a shit—though he suspected that Psycho, deep down, did. (He accused her once of secretly believing in God, which she denied, then admitted, which was hot, and they had sex, sort of.)

The difference between them: She had a deep down, whereas he was all exposed and on the surface. Even now he thought he might shoot her an e-mail. He wanted to be sure she remembered him. He drew a more free-form line down his upper arm with the X-Acto knife and watched the fine line of blood inscribe itself on him, like code.

BABE TRIED, afterward, to analyze what she'd done, what had happened to her beautiful androgynous boy. He'd come out of her sixteen years ago, a new person, and Babe had given him that big-faced, oar-heaving, hard-drinking Nordic name. She didn't blame herself for everything. She'd taken steps to maintain her sanity, her dignity and her self-respect—and left her husband, Bug. Her daughter, Emma, lived on her own, but Babe took Harald with her, and moved to a redwood cabin in a town a few miles away. The school was better, or at least different, and Babe had a job managing a B and B in the town. She did what she had to do, she told her best friend, Georgie. Somebody had to be Harald's mother.

"You are not just his mother," Georgie told her. "You are a human being. You have a *responsibility* to have a life."

Georgie threw a dinner party for Babe and Bug, to acknowledge the change in their lives. Babe's daughter, Emma, came, and so did Harald and his then girlfriend, Psycho. Georgie kept stirring more sugar into a pitcher of bitter Brazilian caipirinhas. She also made a special dish that had been her Syrian grandmother's. She wrung ground lamb with water through her hands until pink water ran into the deep blue bowl, which looked good against the lamb. For the first time, Babe realized, really, what "meat" was—the tender mash of it purified by its water bath. Georgie held out a dime-size bite on a spoon—and Babe ate it.

The Bugmans, a loose confederation of four, gathered as a family for the last time. Georgie fed them a beautiful dinner, then had them all draw Chinese sticks from a beautiful wooden tub. (Everything Georgie owned was beautiful, or turned beautiful in her possession.)

Babe's fortune said she would get an unusual inheritance from a relative, that everything she achieved would come through her work—and she would get her wish. Greedily, Babe chose another Chinese stick, which said a strange dream would come true. Bug's stick read that he would be granted two wishes. He wished for new rotors for his Subaru—and for world peace. Even Harald and Psycho (who didn't reveal their wishes) seemed content with what they got. Georgie read her own stick last. It said, "You will suffer an illness before old age, and only part of your wish will come true."

"Put it back," said Babe. "Take another."

HARALD SLEPT sixteen hours a day. Babe tried to wake him gently for school before she went to work, played classical music on the radio, brought him orange juice, built a fire—but nothing helped. He lied about his meds, hid pills in his socks or saved and took them all at once for a more devastating impact. Maybe she should have done more to give him continuity after the divorce. What should she have done? She'd kept his spaceman sheets.

Their funky handmade cabin in the woods off the 609 was temporary—its most potent charm. Even the outbuilding Babe used as a bedroom had torn slightly away from the hillside. One wall angled obliquely from the floor—six degrees, gauged Harald, a precise and mathematical person. The doors rattled like loose teeth, but Babe slept well here, at first, when she knew her son slept nearby, drugged and safe.

She felt almost happy this way, without anything she wanted. Then she began to have visual hallucinations. Once she thought she awakened to find a Japanese man dressed in a yellow wet suit holding out a mirror. When she looked at her reflection, she found her head covered with eggs—big white chicken eggs. She tried to pull the eggs off her head before they hatched, but they clung to her hair with glue they'd secreted. The Japanese man returned; this time, he wore a blue wet suit. He spoke urgently to Babe in a bubbly, submerged voice she could not understand, but he pulled the eggs from her hair with a tiny red plunger.

Babe believed in work. She'd always worked toward things she wanted. She'd worked on her house, the toy store, her relationship with Bug—all lost now. She used to stay up at night after the children went to bed and paint rooms, work on taxes, read the grand jury report. Even making love with Bug, she'd tick off items on an imaginary list: relieve stress, reconnect, keep balanced. She served her famous marrow jellies to the children, and felt she was building something—bones, muscles, nerve.

Now she lived with Harald, her depressed son, in a

whacked cabin whose water smelled of sulfur and stained all the porcelain black. But the morning fog felt clean. She had a job in town where the owners told her every day how indispensable she was—so indispensable, they didn't give her a day off for four months. Finally, Babe quit, and Aisha, the female partner, responded furiously and refused to pay Babe's back wages.

"How could you do this to us? We depended on you. We *trusted* you," Aisha said. "Now you're stealing the most valuable property we have: our trade secrets."

Aisha glanced at the heavy kerosene ball of the fire lighter by the stone hearth. "If I hear of any other B and B using my cardamom-cinnamon bun recipe, you'll never work in this county again."

Babe said, "If you hit me over the head with that iron ball, I'll come back and haunt you. I'll interfere with the bookings and terrify the guests."

Aisha's gaze wavered. Her weakness: ADHD.

"Call the police, get a restraining order," Aisha told her husband. "Write down the threats she just made." Babe realized that Aisha always took this peremptory tone with him, and wondered what was wrong with the husband, why he stood it.

"Don't bother," Babe said. "I'll go."

She drove home feeling virtuous and free. On the hill outside town, a new couple had brought in African animals— gazelles, elands and zebras. Babe almost hit another car head-on from craning her neck to look at their rare beauty.

The antlers on the elands looked hand-carved. Somebody else must have been distracted, too, because just a few hundred yards up the road, three turkey vultures rose reluctantly from the parallel yellow lines, hovered heavily before her windshield and then moved to the side, revealing the carcass of a fox whose face they'd licked clean as a spoon. She smelled rain and eucalyptus on the air, and rushed home. Maybe she'd bake those cardamom-cinnamon buns for Harald, fill the house with a rich, comforting atmosphere. When she arrived, though, she found—literally—a dark cloud over her house. Sometimes life's perverse, Babe thought. You find yourself, which means someone else gets lost.

HARALD WROTE his name in blood on his arm, then drank three-quarters of a bottle of white rum and e-mailed his ex-girlfriend Psycho a long, guilt-tripping letter about his meaningless life. Although he didn't confess exactly what he'd done, the letter was so long and rambling, she put two and two together and called the sheriff, and an hour later the deputy came. Harald, unconscious, did not respond. The deputy opened the front door (unlocked) and found Harald lying quietly on his back, bleeding hard from both arms into the bedding. The deputy said it looked like a murder scene.

The paramedics bandaged Harald's arms and head. (He'd fallen and gouged his temple; at first, the gouge seemed more serious than the slashed arms and the alcohol poisoning.) The ambulance drove him two and a half hours to a psychiatric hospital, which someone called "the Bug House." Babe almost laughed when she heard that—"the Bug House." Not that it was funny.

She felt afraid to visit her son there, afraid of seeing him for what he was—a scar. His arms were marked so that he would never again have real privacy around his body; any stranger could read on his arms what he'd done. He didn't want to see her anyway. He felt, the head nurse said stiffly, "quite violent about it." So Babe drove home. A black widow spider lived in the jamb of the front door; she had to open the door carefully or she would kill it.

Her eyes wouldn't close when she lay down, so she had a lot of time to clean. The cabin sparkled pointlessly. She hung up kitschy stuff, Madonna night-lights, a portrait Harald had done in high school of Christ represented as a gopher on a cross. She carried wood and kindling, split logs, swept pine needles off the little decks, made altars out of pinecones and broken necklaces. When she finished this work, she started on the stones. She moved one up from the ravine onto the deck. It was an unusual stone—larger than most, smoother, whiter. It had holes bored into it that certain mollusks make. Then she found another stone, and then another; it was like finding mushrooms—once you knew how to look, you saw them everywhere.

She brought stones inside and put them away. Moving stones made her tired, and after she worked she slept.

*   *   *

IN ONE OF her vivid reveries, Babe met a rock star as he drove toward the highway in a low-slung sports car, a vintage Corvette. Babe walked along the road, gathering stones, and the rock star pulled up alongside her and rolled his window down. "I have a cabin," he told her. "I hardly ever use it. Go down there whenever you want and hang loose."

Babe walked farther down the road. Immediately the landscape changed and became wild. Vultures circled overhead. Sharp rocks jutted up fifty feet into a sky that glowed yellow, like the moon. A small reptilian animal chased her, baring its sharp teeth. Babe knew that the animal would attack, and it did: It charged and bit her hand. The wound left a trail of blood behind her, but now the terrible thing Babe had known would happen had happened, and she could relax. The mad animal seemed calmer, too. They walked down the road together like old friends, but no cabin waited at the end where Babe could hang loose.

SOME EVENINGS, she carried only three or four stones up the ravine. She piled them on the fireplace or used one to hold down a stack of bills on a table. Other times, she gathered more and stored them around the house. One day, she filled the whole fireplace with stones. Then—because she could use the outdoor shower—she filled the bathtub. Sometimes she couldn't help herself. Sometimes she felt ashamed. She carried stones into her house the way people drank or did junk. She thought about not doing it; sometimes she stopped for a few hours or a day and began to feel calm and free. But then the day darkened and she went outside, imagining herself simply going out to gather firewood, knowing that a fire was impossible. Just the weight of the stones in her hands, in her house, comforted her. From the void of black space where she lived (in her body), they brought her, even, to the edge of bliss.

AS A LITTLE BOY, Harald used to climb into her bed in the evenings to read. Once, when she asked him why, he said, "Because it's warm." Babe said, "We haven't been in bed for fifteen hours!" And Harald shrugged and said, "It's *still* warm."

More recently, Babe remembered his brown eyes looking up at her from over the top of some book—*Nausea*, by Jean-Paul Sartre, or *The Sorrows of Young Werther*, by Goethe, or *Pain, Sex and Time*, by Gerald Heard, or *Astrophysics of Gaseous Nebulae*, by whomever—the humor there, the bit of perversity. He said, "Mom, you should smile more."

Babe yelled, "Are you kidding? I am the only person in this family who smiles every single day! I smile at customers! I smile at you!"

Harald said, "No, I mean you should smile—for fun." And he smiled his dazzling rare smile, because he'd caught her shouting, at the end of her rope.

*   *   *

ONE AFTERNOON, Georgie called and asked how Harald was doing in the hospital. "About as badly as possible," said Babe. "What else is new?"

Georgie said, "I found out this morning that I have breast cancer." When Georgie said the words *breast cancer,* Babe looked at the stone in her hand—a five-pounder. A window closed, leaving just a tiny aperture through which Babe saw her hand and the stone in her hand.

"Left-handed women are more likely to get it," Georgie went on in a clinical voice. "Something to do with asymmetry in the female, more hormones gathering in vessels on the left side, near the spleen. The left arm acts as a kind of hormone switch, turning the estrogen off and on."

"Who told you that?" asked Babe.

"I was up all night, reading."

Babe thought of Georgie's left hand always in motion, setting type, scissoring a chicken up its back, stirring up a pitcher of caipirinhas. Writing a list, Georgie held her pen in that protective way lefties do. Chopping an onion or writing a letter or deadheading her roses, Georgie switched the chemical sauna on and off.

"What are you going to do?" Babe asked.

"What else can I do? Raw foods, single-malt scotch, surgery, radiation and chemotherapy. I'm going to do it all." Georgie laughed a gutsy, throaty laugh, like an old lounge singer. "Oh, but wait, do you want to hear the best part?"

"Hit me," said Babe.

"They create the new one while you're still on the operating table. They use your own love handles, can you believe it? The larger your love handles, the bigger the boobs."

Georgie sounded tough over the phone, and Babe, scared and horrified, laughed with her. She remembered later how hard and loudly they laughed at how tough they were going to be.

THE BOUNDARY

*S*carface was obnoxious, but he had charisma. The first time I met him, he showed me a coffee can with dead tadpoles in the bottom. He offered to sell them—with the coffee can—for ten dollars. I drove him home from Madrigal to the rez. He asked if, when I bought my car, it came with the engine. I said the car came with the engine. Then he asked whether it came with the key.

I admired his directness. "Listen, you're a hippie," he said. "Can you get me some weed?"

"You want me to get you some weed."

"If you get me some weed, I can get you commodities. Peanut butter, apple juice, powdered eggs—whatever you want."

"Dream on," I said.

"If you get me weed, I'll make you *breakfast,* you know what I mean?" Scarface smiled benignly.

I didn't answer. How could I? He was only twelve. Just outside town, I turned up a stretch of road that ran through hills and gullies that bloomed with wild mustard and fennel and cow parsnip and the carcasses of American-made cars named after wild horses. One end of this road opened at the rez, with its HUD houses and rosebushes, where Scarface lived. On the other end stood the Assembly of God. In between, we passed a ranch where a wealthy couple from Los Angeles had brought hundreds of rare wild birds. Immediately the turkey farm across the road sued them for bringing in exotic bird diseases, and someone shot their dogs.

"You saying I'm ugly?" Scarface shouted suddenly. "Huh? 'Cause I'm packing heat!" He pointed to his penis.

This was a test. Sure, Scarface was ugly, as enormous and threatening as possible for a person his age, not yet full-grown. His face looked like a knife wound. But beautiful, too.

"I have to keep my eyes on the road," I lied.

"If you get me some weed, I'll forgive white people for all the injustices done to Indians," he said.

"Scarface," I said, "how can you forgive white people?"

He looked out the window at the dusty plain of the turkey farm and said, "If I didn't know how to forgive people, I wouldn't have no family or friends."

It was true. Scarface's own father had shot and killed two men in a state of such profound drunkenness that at the trial he could not recall the crime, the men or his reasons. He lived in prison—the worst one. Scarface's mother did odd jobs with men.

Scarface couldn't really read—he spelled his own name "Scrafac" on a piece of paper he gave me with his telephone number on it. I don't know what they did with him in fifth grade; he still held the pencil in his fist. I would have liked to take Scarface away and make him mine—but you can't do that. Whatever my reasons were for wanting Scarface, they were the wrong reasons. I bought him pickles and jerky and doughnut holes at the gas station, and loved him the way you might love someone for his money or his beauty.

AROUND THE TIME I started my gig with Artists in the Schools and got to know Scarface—the year of my messy and depressing separation—my sister, Carrie, called from the Democratic Republic of the Congo, where she'd been teaching in a private school. Her life, she said, had become worthwhile and exciting. She'd forgiven me for being one of the neglectful figures from her childhood. In fact, she invited me to come and visit. She spoke of the political situation; after the most recent eruptions, the State Department began to worry about all her "kids"—diplomats' children and children of the ruling families—being sitting ducks, but all they did, at the school, was to postpone a field trip to the capital, where rape and machetes were "of concern."

"That sounds dangerous," I said.

"We went to see the bonobos instead," said Carrie.

A few weeks later, Carrie called again to say she'd been evacuated and had moved to another country in Africa, where she was doing important work with Doctors Without Borders, treating girls and women with fistulas, ruptures and internal damage from rape, long labors in childbirth, or babies too big for the child-size birth canals of the youngest or most malnourished girls. This damage had rendered many incontinent; they'd lost the wall between vagina and anus, and lived in shame.

"You should come," Carrie said. "Then you'd see."

SCARFACE KNEW about bonobos from watching the Discovery Channel. Bonobos were his favorite kind of ape. They could pick up a teacup with their toes and drink from it. They didn't force the females to have sex with them—they fucked equally and by agreement. Scarface put a bonobo in the mural even though we'd agreed not to deviate too much from the sketches we'd made, or from our local history theme. We'd agreed to depict salmon and kelp, redwoods and round houses, Pomo women weaving baskets from redbud and willow and men dressed for dancing in flicker headbands and feather skirts. Painting the mural was supposed to help kids like Scarface reclaim their own narratives. (I'd written these words myself in several successful grant proposals.) The city had agreed that we could use the wall of the Lions Club for the mural, but then it immediately granted a permit for the medical center next door to expand into the parking lot.

A truck brought in three modular buildings in one day,

creating an alley between the medical center and the mural. The public would never see our work; on the other hand, we had a county grant and artistic freedom.

I wanted to bring the mural into the present tense, break down some of the old romanticized imagery. There weren't even any redwoods on the rez; it was a floodplain. Scarface had probably seen more bonobos on the Discovery Channel than salmon in the Rez River. I told the kids, "Paint what you see around you, not what people tell you is there." One of the kids put in his grandma on kidney dialysis, smoking a pipe. Another contributed a kitchen sink with brown water running out of it. On Tuesday and Thursday afternoons, we painted in the shadows. At night, kids sold drugs and drank beer around the mural. I think they were drawn by the liminal quality of the space, and by the mural itself, which every day became more complicated, beautiful and hard to read.

Scarface didn't like to take the late bus—kids teased him about the men who climbed in through his mother's bedroom window—so after we worked on the mural, I drove him home. One time, we talked about the mural and the bonobos; then Scarface shared some letters he said his girlfriend, Maria, had written to him. I probably shouldn't have let him go on, but his confidence and expression amazed me. Wasn't Scarface supposed to be illiterate?

"You read those well," I said finally, and he said, "Well, I already *know* what they say."

I pulled into his driveway. A dog stood on a car's roof in the yard, barking. A girl also stood in the yard, staring up into a pine tree. She had a round face and a round body and very long black hair that had been oiled for lice and pulled back into a bun. Her eyes were brown and deep. "My cousin," Scarface explained. "Maria."

"Scarface," the girl shouted, "your big brother threw my *thong* up in that tree."

"Why don't you climb up and get it?" he asked.

"You don't know what's been in that tree," Maria said, and grinned.

Scarface flashed me a beautiful smile from his ugly mug and slammed the car door behind him.

THE LAST TIME my sister came to visit, she rode my bicycle into town every day and leaned it up against a tree behind the coffeehouse where she spent her mornings writing e-mail and opening up her heart to the regulars. Carrie has always impressed people with her stories and with her résumé, which she can recite like a villanelle. She suffered damage as a child from having been kissed and fondled by an uncle, which led to her radical identification with the oppressed. She worked at a rape crisis center and a suicide hot line, then put herself through nursing and business school, overcame asthma and anorexia, studied French, and became the crusader she is today. Carrie's lived and worked in seven countries, four of them in Africa. We've had different experiences, different lives, Carrie and I. Carrie says no, we just have different versions of reality.

I asked if she locked it—the bike—and she said, "The trouble with you is that you have no faith in people." When someone finally stole the bike, she called me for a ride home and refused to go back to my "low-life" town. Carrie's like that—rigid, unilateral.

Love is a degraded word. I love my coffee in the morning. I love sunsets and those arias from Handel's operas—*Agrippina, Atalanta, Lotario, Samson*—sung by Renée Fleming that my ex-husband turned me on to. I feel a complicated mix of ambivalent affections for my sister, but the truth is, I have never loved her, didn't even when we were children.

Our uncle Gene, a policeman, caused a scandal, statutory, which infected our whole family before my sister and I were born. He lost his job, and even did time in prison. When my sister was coming up, three years behind me, nobody wanted to open old wounds. Uncle Gene wasn't young or handsome or powerful anymore. Carrie was large and quick enough to defend herself—or, it was felt, she should have been. Even now the words my sister uses to describe her life—*molested, abandoned, alone, exposed*—sound exaggerated. My sister always seemed dull and literal to me; I loved intrigue and secrets.

Uncle Gene died of a gangrenous leg in Aunt Bea's living room. Aunt Bea was much older than she had expected to be when he died—but still relieved. Within a month, though, she stopped breathing fluently and had to drag around a small oxygen tank. She said, "I know it sounds pathetic, but all I really want is a cigarette."

From Aunt Bea I learned that you could hate your life and still love life.

As far as I know, Uncle Gene never *forced* anybody to do anything. But he was persuasive. He made girls feel something, and when they were really feeling it, Uncle Gene was there with his avuncular touch. He was, of course, a bad man. But just as great individuals are sometimes scarred by flaws, can't a bad man be varnished by qualities?

Because of my experiences with Uncle Gene (the playful banter, the pressure and push-back, the tickling, the touching, the lap-sits, the terrible, interesting frankness of his desire), I understand boundaries and enjoy controlling them. Because of him, I'm not afraid of red zones in human relations, just as my sister is drawn to her African hot spots.

In the mural, I gave Uncle Gene a cameo, a little piece of the action, even though he isn't part of local history. I painted him lying on his back with his arms spread out, very flat and stylized, completely open. I could have emphasized his vulnerability, or punished him in some way, had his liver pecked at by ravens. But what interests me about this uncle is not his amorality—it's his freedom.

SCARFACE HAD BEEN ASKING since September what I was going to buy him for Christmas. "Jews don't celebrate Christmas," I told him.

"But *I* celebrate Christmas," Scarface said. "And what I'd really like is a bag of weed."

Just before winter break, I arranged to take my students to the city for a day—a two-plus hour drive—to see the murals in the library, city hall, and a mosque. It turned out everyone had a grant for a mural; everyone had a narrative they needed to reclaim.

No one showed up except Scarface, so we drove down together. At the library, we walked through a detecting machine. "It's to make sure you aren't walking away with a book that isn't checked out," I explained.

Scarface looked incredulous. "Who'd jack a book?" he asked.

At city hall, he walked confidently up to the metal detector, and when it went off, he levitated three feet, turned in midair and bolted. I found him out front, sitting on the rear bumper of a black limousine with embassy plates.

"What's wrong?" I asked.

"You said they checked you for books."

"That one's a metal detector. To check you for guns."

"Or *knives*," Scarface said, brandishing his.

We watched together as a beautiful woman walked down the staircase, wearing a long dress of cream-colored satin and carrying a bouquet of roses.

"Bitch looks like an angel," Scarface said.

We strolled through alleyways in the Mission, observing the iconography of the murals. Scarface peppered me with questions about urban life. When you bought coffee in a restaurant, did you get all the milk and the sugar you wanted? When you bought a house, did it come with electricity? When you bought life insurance, could you kill yourself? When you bought stocks, like Coke, did you get Coke for free? If one of those johns paid you to lie down, could you get your nut off, too?

I thought, This must be what it is like to have a child. Not that I wanted a child, but it was nice, walking around with a kid asking question after question, expressing curiosity.

In the mosque, we ran into a stampede of empty shoes on the mint green rug. Men prostrated themselves, or leaned up against the walls, or knelt before the Imam, who spoke rapidly in Arabic about moderation, modesty and patience. Scarface and I sat in back with an interpreter, who wore a headset and translated what the Imam said. Men came and went freely, clasping the hands of their brothers as they passed while putting the other hand over their heart—a formal yet intimate gesture.

I joined the women in a separate, closed-off room where we could hear the Imam but not distract or be seen by him. Handwritten flyers pasted to the walls admonished us in English not to whisper during prayers. Nevertheless, the women introduced themselves in whispers. One was an Austrian who had converted; another was Apache from the Southwest. The Apache woman had just converted last Thursday, and she wished everyone in the world the same happiness she had found in Islam. A high school senior said Islam gave her a beautiful privacy. She was not oppressed or forced to choose.

The mural itself was disappointing—the usual romantic imagery: camels. City kids had done it, but everything about the mural spoke to a distant past in the desert.

The mosque served a free lunch—cumin rice and falafel, chopped salad, and baklava. Somebody opened up the soda machine at the front of the mosque and handed out free sodas. Scarface was impressed, and he drank two Cokes.

"I want to be a Muslim," he said.

"Why?" I asked.

"I like these guys because they scare the white guys."

"You want to scare people?"

"I already scare people," Scarface pointed out. "And I know how to pray."

When we reached the car, somebody had broken the small rear window. The backseat was covered with glass.

"Why did they go in the back window?" I wondered aloud.

"They didn't want to make too much noise," Scarface said.

"They didn't even take the stereo. They only took my fleece jacket—but it had sixty dollars in the pocket."

"Sixty bucks would be enough," he said with a tone that indicated I was a snob.

He swept the broken glass into a piece of the cardboard and dumped it carefully down a sewer grate while I taped up the back window with strips of duct tape left over from my marriage, when I'd been prepared for everything. While

Scarface cut tape off the roll with his knife, he noticed a transgender woman in a blue dress and high heels crossing the street. "Jesus, what is that?" he said, grabbing my arm.

"That's a man who is taking hormones to make him look and feel more like a woman," I told him.

"I never saw anything like that before," he said. "I do not approve of that."

"Oh, come on," I said. "Lighten up."

"You approve of that?" Scarface asked, loudly enough for the transgender woman to hear. I saw, suddenly, what the transperson saw, a big kid, probably with a knife.

"Of course I approve," I said loudly.

We didn't speak again until we drove over the bridge and Scarface told me he was carsick. I took a detour to Mount Tam, and we talked and walked up a wide dirt path, higher and higher.

"So can anyone just go to San Francisco?" he asked.

"It's a free country," I said.

"Is Los Angeles in America?" Scarface wanted to go there. He wanted to know if it was true that Juvie, where his older brother went, was a town run by Jews.

"No—it stands for juvenile," I said. "Kids."

"So where are the Jews?"

"Jews live everywhere. In diaspora."

"Did somebody take their land?"

"Usually, yeah," I said.

"That's exactly what happened to Indians," said Scarface. "That's why I could never be racist against Jews like my mom is."

"There's Israel, but it's small, and other people were living there, too."

"Do the Jews have an army?"

"In Israel, they have a pretty good one."

"That's what I mean, man. Motherfuckers can't *mess* with their land."

"Well, and there are all these different tribes of Jews, like Native Americans, and everybody's mixed up, too, like on the rez. My mother was Jewish; my father wasn't. My sister isn't. I am—but I don't even believe in God."

"How can you not believe in God? That's fucked-up! What stops you from doing something bad?"

"You can't just be a good person because you think God is watching—"

"Sure you can," Scarface said gently, his voice encouraging.

IF SOMEONE surgically removed my memories and let me keep one, this might be it—this day—though it was probably a mistake to take him on a four-mile round-trip hike. We started in a black blanket of fog and climbed up a steep grade on a gravelly path toward blue sky. Half a mile up, Scarface was sweating. It hadn't occurred to me that he could be out of shape. "What's the matter?" I asked.

"I've got asthma and bronchitis," he said.

"Really?"

"Yeah. And I'm obese."

A couple wearing spandex shorts and shirts rode past us on thousand-dollar bicycles. "This reminds me of the time I climbed Masada," one of them said.

"Hey, could I have a swig of your water?" Scarface shouted at the bicyclists. The couple pedaled faster.

"I'm just messing witchou!" he yelled after them.

I practically pushed him to the top, but we made it. I wanted this success, I thought, for Scarface. Before he filed for divorce, my ex-husband used to tell me that I always try to extract more from an experience than is there to be withdrawn.

When we reached the top, Scarface wasn't really able to talk anymore, and by the time we'd hiked two miles back to the car, the sky was dark. I'd planned to get him home at a reasonable hour. His mother wasn't exactly overprotective, but she was still a mother.

SCARFACE STOPPED WORKING on the mural. He just stopped coming. I drove out to his house. The little dog still stood barking on the roof of the car, but no one answered when I knocked on the door. Finally, I called Mr. Boyle, the county administrator in charge of the mural project, who read Scarface's accusation: " 'I was the only kid on the field trip. It wasn't even a field trip. It was just me.' "

Mr. Boyle said, "I can't believe you don't know even common-monsense things—don't drive the kids alone, for example. Didn't you read the guidelines?"

"Guidelines for what? What guidelines?" I asked.

"The guidelines on the Web site," Mr. Boyle said. "The kid was pretty specific. It would be hard to make up the stuff he was saying—a kid like him, on a learning plan, pretty high special needs. It might be impossible to make up."

"To make up what?"

"The pornographic imagery."

"What pornographic imagery?"

"Did you climb up a tree to retrieve your undergarments?"

"No—that was his cousin."

Mr. Boyle said, "Look, it's not that I have any reason to believe him. It's that I don't have any reason to believe you. I'm old. I don't believe anybody."

Scarface remained in the mural, though, digging in a hole in the ground, unearthing relics from the past—an old Coke bottle, an arrowhead, a coffee can, a safety razor. New kids joined the project and helped. "Paint what you see," I told them. "Don't just paint stuff people tell you is there."

I even had new favorites, smart, assertive kids—Javier, Alicia, Salvador, Nick—who basically just needed an adult to say their names and mean it.

THEN AUNT BEA DIED and left me a little money. I took every penny and booked a trip to Africa to visit Carrie over the spring break. At first, I hardly recognized my sister: She looked like a nun. Her face had the planes and angles of a clenched fist, especially under the white hat she wore. The dry air and exposure to injustice had puckered her like a raisin. She despised America—she was full of good and subtle reasons—though she remained hopeful about the beneficial effects of free-market capitalism on the local economy.

Carrie lived, with a few others like her, in a hut made of sticks and grass. Her hut smelled of the powdery body spray she's used since she was nine. It smelled of my sister—damp, sweet, childish, chemical. I kept a journal of my impressions, as if I might be responsible for making a mural of the visit. Unfortunately, I made only two entries before I got sick.

Noted
date and mangrove trees
early human remains
special volumizing shampoo
erg: sea of sand in the desert
reg: gravel-covered plain
antimalarial drugs, sunscreen
1 bottle Russian vodka
Percocet, Welbutrin
main sources of water: dew and fog
oil reserves

Noted

C. surrounded by girls twelve, thirteen, fourteen years
old, whose babies ripped apart their child-size organs, or
whose organs were ripped apart in other ways. Girls wait
for doctor without borders to sew them up. One doctor,
seventy girls; doctor travels from village to village. C.'s
proj. can be expressed in algorithms of futility. Buttery
Dutch doctor emerges from grass house after every fourth
or fifth procedure in foul mood. Can't blame him.

C. wears white lab coat over jeans—perfect sepia
handprint on sleeve. Girls crowd around. Most will never
get repairs. Doctor will move to next village; girls will
return to margins of home, irritating their husbands and
parents, who are embarrassed they exist.

Every time C. calls a name, ten girls shuffle forward,
dribble pools of fluid. Their calves, under bright batik
skirts, shine. Seventy girls came, equal in despair. A few
now less desperate than the others. Those chosen do not
show that they're glad.

C. loves this work. Also think she loves the doctor without
borders.

In the evening, we sat under Carrie's mosquito net and
drank quinine water mixed with her vodka. Carrie didn't

want to talk about the girls or the doctor. She wanted to talk about childhood things, especially Uncle Gene. "Did he ever ask if he could kiss you?" Again, she wanted to know. An ammonia scent clung to her, bringing back a vivid memory of what my sister was to me as a small child—a pissy smell, a drag.

"What do you want me to say? Uncle Gene was a lech— yes, yes, yes, yes, yes," I said. This line of questioning has always seemed to me beside the point. I hate when people identify their whole lives with their dysfunctional families; I refuse to be defined by mine.

"But you admitted yourself—"

"No, I didn't. Nothing terrible happened to me."

"For me, every day is like it just happened," she said.

"What happened, Carrie?"

"He pressured me. He kissed me and he touched my breast. It went on for years. Nobody wanted to hear it. You know this."

"What do you want, Carrie? Everyone is dead—Gene, Auntie, our parents."

"I want you to acknowledge what happened to us."

"You make it sound like the Holocaust," I said.

"You minimize it because you liked it," she said.

We'd said all these words before.

Her face conveyed intense dry rays of heat. "I knew you'd come because you've made a mess of your own life," she said. "But your denial is disgusting and insane."

I felt dehydrated, sunstruck. This must have been the

illness coming on. A day later, I was chilled and shaking; then for an indefinite time I was just alive instead of dead. Existence became a dim red point of light; when I put my hand over my heart, the light went out. Carrie stood behind a yellow haze, as remote as a figure projected onto a movie screen. I felt no hope at all. But I did not die.

Time moved backward and forward. I asked Carrie for an egg. She laughed bitterly. The U.S.-owned oil giant had promised to create model chicken farms, so that the community could be self-sustaining. But those in the community did not want to take the chicken coop–building workshop. They wanted the oil giant to build the chicken coops. As a result of the impasse, the chickens grew sick and died. The eggs, my sister told me, still lay in their cradles of hay. Did I want one?

The doctor without borders came. He asked Carrie for a cup of tea. From his tone, I understood that the two of them were sleeping together. In a fever, you see things. The day Uncle Gene died, his face appeared to me in a dream.

Carrie slid a bedpan under my hip. "You're really sick, you know," she said. She brought a bottle of pills and left it on the table beside my little bed of straw. "You can have them all," I think she said.

"I can't take pills," I told her.

"Suit yourself," she said, and set a glass of water down on the table so hard that the glass cracked up the side.

Her ministrations continued while I went in and out. She boiled a chicken—head and feathers and all. We sat in a formal dining room before our mother's Spode soup plates. My plate contained the whole chicken, the feathers drenched and steaming. Carrie sat at the opposite end of the table, drinking a glass of water.

"You have to choose," she said. "Eat—or die."

I picked up my fork and knife and began to eat. Although the chicken was poisonous, it was also delicious, and made me stronger. In this way, my sister saved my life.

THE ACCIDENT HAPPENED on my birthday, a stormy night in January. My friend Georgie gave a small dinner party. We had champagne in flutes, raw ahi on thin slices of cucumber, then chicken pie and mustard greens. We told bawdy stories and listened to Portuguese fado. I wore a black silk camisole under an old wool sweater. Georgie and I both dressed in this absurd but comfortable way after our marriages broke up, and I think it had to do with feeling, as we did, hot and cold at the same time.

When the power went out, someone opened another bottle of wine. Just then, Georgie's ex-husband, who is a first responder, came in, peeling off his yellow reflective coat. We cried out gaily, "Did anything terrible happen?"

"You don't want to know," he said, and we grew sober for a moment, imagining what.

Georgie calls her ex—Carl—a superhero. Carl *is* a super-hero: humble, strong, brave, not too emotional. These qualities, which initially drew her to him, eventually turned into the reasons she left him—though they stayed friends.

Carl washed his hands, drank his wine, and tucked into his chicken pie.

"Two rez kids, probably doing a hundred miles an hour. The driver was just thirteen years old—he's survived, so far. The other kid was thrown across the river. They can't even tell if it's a boy or a girl."

MY KIDS WERE WORKING on a new project now—flags for the main street of the town. At first when I heard them talking, I thought Scarface was the one killed in the crash. But the kid who died was his cousin, Maria. Scarface had the wheel.

How could I have forgotten? It had been nine months since I'd seen him. It was toward the end of school; I'd come back from Africa and finished the mural. Somebody had painted over the bonobo and replaced it with some generic ravens circling a roundhouse. The grandma on dialysis was still there, smoking her pipe; so was Uncle Gene, on his back, facing the sky. I went to the district office to pick up my check, and when I came out, the kids were walking to their buses, and there was Scarface, taller and fatter than I remembered. I walked him to his bus, a distance of thirty feet. We didn't talk. He climbed on the bus and walked to the back row, where the Indian kids sat, stone-faced and silent. I called after him, "Hey, Scarface, have a good summer." Nothing. I climbed the three steps into the bus and yelled down the aisle, "Hey, Scarface, have a good summer!"

"You were going to get me some weed!" he shouted, his voice full of rage and hope.

I backed up and almost fell out of the bus. The driver unfolded the yellow doors and took him away. My sister would say I have a hardened, ruined heart, and maybe it's true. I'd blocked him from my mind.

ISLE OF WIGS

*S*ura asked a red-faced woman. She asked a high school track star. She asked a woman who stole three lollipops from the front desk and held them unrepentantly, like cigarettes. She asked a Buddhist monk. She asked a man. Everybody said the same: The Isle of Wigs—go there.

It was on Wilshire, not far from DuPar's, and she stopped first and had a pancake to steel herself. She bought one wig the first day and then went back a couple of weeks later and bought another. Two wigs turned out to be a minimum. Should she buy more? Sura couldn't believe insurance wouldn't cover a head of hair. If she lost a finger, wouldn't insurance cover it? If she lost a ring? The faith healer her son Daniel found through the gym wasn't covered, either. Plus, he was a Catholic, which made Sura wonder what her own mother, dead of the same disease for thirty years, would think. Would she be happy or even more furious to see her daughter saved by that kind of faith?

When her son bought her a German alarm clock so she wouldn't be late for all her appointments, Sura took it right back to Longs to exchange it for an American item. But the bright aisles distracted her (she needed a new bath mat, measuring cups, spot remover, a replacement head for her electric toothbrush—they wanted *ten* dollars, but you could buy two for seventeen). Toys reminded her of the grandchildren she didn't have yet; perfumes reminded her of old, sick women, and cameras and film reminded her of the boxes of unsorted pictures in her garage in the desert that showed the arc of her life so far. Nothing reminded her of her mission until, back in the parking lot, she reached into her purse for her car keys and found the black clock ticking.

TIME! Sura's children said she wasted her time, looking through the paper every day at the sales in stores when, for her own peace of mind, she should be putting her affairs in order. But what was she supposed to do about the bonds and certificates? Should she pay down the mortgage, pay the taxes? It was a terrible mess and nobody could help her, nobody. Her neighborhood association had called, sorry about her personal setbacks, but it had to cite her for unwatered landscaping. The Rosens had put green rocks in their yard; somebody else had paved theirs all over with Astroturf. It didn't look bad—and compared to the expense of plants!

Sura was supposed to find an hour a day to relax and visualize health, then fertilize the orange trees, but who could do so much?

"Every day you're not in chemotherapy is a day wasted," the nurse in Dr. Frank's office told her, adding to the pressure. But you couldn't have chemotherapy every day.

At the infusion center (twenty minutes late), she arranged herself in one of the titan-size pink Barcaloungers, which reminded Sura of pedicures at the Waxing Manicure—improving forces. All you had to do was lie back. The good nurse, Julie, sunk a needle into the port in her chest, which Dr. Frank said wouldn't hurt after the first time, but it did. Why wouldn't it? It throbbed like a heart, demanded attention like a child. Sura dozed—*they put drugs in the chemo to keep you quiet*—and found herself beyond the padded chair, in the jungle with a dirt floor and a green smell among wild animals too busy with their own animal lives to hurt her. A black chimpanzee lay on his back while his mate pulled fleas or lice from his ear with her thick human fingers. Sura opened her eyes and closed them again—not dreaming, just thinking. Last summer, she'd studied Ape Language & Culture with her best friend, Sophie, at the Elderhostel in Seattle. The food was to die for. The famous Jewish poet Allen Ginsberg's mother had been there—nice lady, Naomi Ginsberg. ("Allen Ginsberg's mother died in 1956," her son told Sura, always eager to *specifically* contradict her, although where was he in 1956? Unborn!) Sura had sat next to Naomi the night they watched a film in which monkeys swung from manzanita branches, babies clinging for their lives to the hairy breasts. But an awful thing happened in Seattle: Sophie died—a heart attack in the dining room.

Sura woke horribly chilled in her chemo chair, cisplatin dripping into the port in her chest, to find that the technician with one eye had given her snack to an older, sicker woman who seemed confused—by America, Sura guessed.

"Why did you give her my snack?" Sura asked.

"You were sleeping so nicely," the technician said meanly.

"I had a nightmare!" Sura told her.

A little stick figure—the good nurse, Julie—brought Sura orange juice and a cookie, chatted about her vacation coming up. Her husband wanted to take her to the Panama Canal, even though she'd been there already during a different marriage. Sura frowned and said, "Why don't you go to Israel?"

"Barry doesn't want to go to Israel. He's had two heart attacks already, and he says, 'I want to see the Panama Canal before I die.' What am I going to do? Besides, they're fighting in Israel. It isn't a good time."

"They're always fighting," Sura told her. "It's never a good time. But when you go, you'll see—it's a good time." She hadn't been since 1972. Now who knew when she'd go back?

SURA COULDN'T SHOP after chemo—she went home and went to bed—but the next afternoon she drove to Home Depot and picked out forty dollars' worth of hot-weather blooms, showy things that looked good right now, but tomorrow, who knew? She'd rushed out in a hurry, put a pink bandanna on her head; she was bald as an egg. The woman who rang her up, gorgeous girl, thirty years old, winked at Sura and picked up her hair for a second as if it were a hat.

"Oh my God," Sura said.

Forty dollars was the least of it. She didn't even have the energy to call the handyman to ask him to come and put in the plants. The chemo brought her platelets down. She tried to eat half a bagel and a little spinach salad and read the newspaper—but it made her sick, looking at the pictures from Israel of the blown-up bus. People talking as if they were used to it, as if they could accept such a dangerous life. No! She would not accept it. The twelve-year-old boy carried off in Gaza by his schoolmates, his eyes rolled up into his head. His friends with their book bags still on their backs! One boy hung behind, maybe scared the same thing could happen to him. When Sophie died, Sura hung behind also, even though she was Sophie's oldest and best friend, the only person who knew her well. One minute Sophie was standing beside Sura in the buffet line, saying, "Look, corn bread!" and the next she was lying unconscious on the floor. Sura would never forget what she saw—a pulmonary embolism. An ambulance took Sophie away and an hour later she was dead. Sura hung behind, not out of meanness, just an instinct.

Dr. Frank's office called, trying to change her next

appointment for sooner. "What, he's going out of town?" Sura asked the receptionist.

"No, no."

"So he thinks I'm not going to make it to Thursday?" She shifted her weight on her puffy slippers, but wrote the new date down on her calendar, inked thickly already with appointments with Dr. Frank and the clinic and the periodontist—teeth were important, the only part of her skeleton that showed—and her childrens' birthdays, just a year and a week apart. Both Daniel and Fay were over forty and neither had children yet. Late, late!

In planning mode, still by the phone, Sura called the handyman, Ramiro. When he came a few hours later, Sura explained that she wanted him to dig up all the dirt in front of the house and lay black plastic under the white rock to keep the weeds down. *Not too much dirt,* she told him in her Spanish. (Actually, she said *not too much thing,* pointing to the dirt. It was hard to get through.) *Sí, sí, señora,* Ramiro told her, and then went away without doing any work at all.

"I don't have much time!" she called after him.

She walked down the hall to her bedroom in her slippers, her hemorrhoids burning and jarring on the concrete slab with the Mexican pavers on top, which had seemed like an attractive idea at the time. She lay down on her bed with her hands at her sides, put earphones in her ears and switched on her relaxation tape. "You are walking on a beautiful beach along the ocean," the reader said. "A fresh breeze is blowing. The breeze smells of fresh air and flowers. Feel the fresh air enter your nose and bring relaxation to your whole head. Feel your eyes relax. Feel your nose relax. Feel your mouth relax. . . . " The port hummed in her chest. Sura hated the beach; the salt made her hair frizz. But now—she had no hair. Sura closed her eyes, folded her hands over her heart and slept.

She woke up with blue-green, mustard-colored nausea floating in front of her eyes. Her daughter, Fay, had told her she should smoke some marijuana.

"Oh my God," Sura had said, astonished. "You want me to get lung cancer, too?" But did Fay listen? She brought two marijuana brownies in a Baggie, which Sura stowed in the back of the freezer. She'd never eat them, but she didn't want Fay to be tempted, either.

She studied a yellow-blue hematoma on her arm. The technician with one eye who took her blood had made it; Sura had never trusted that one. Who ever heard of a technician with one eye? The other eye was glass, always looking away from you. (You expect people with some terrible affliction to be kinder, Sura thought. But why should they be?)

And speaking of trust and her children, when they came to visit, they brought gifts she didn't need or want, and her son stole things, as if she were already dead. From the big box in the garage he stole the best picture of her ever, posing with her husband Nat's big pumpkins that year. He also stole the biggest letter she'd ever gotten. It was from Nat when he served in the army, typed on a special big typewriter on special extra-big paper, two feet wide and three feet long. The letter began "Dearest Heart of Mine, I am about to start the largest letter of my career," and went on about how it was too late for her to turn back, plans had been made (his plans!), the tickets bought. It was a young man's letter, filled with so much language of love she had to make *XXXXXXX*'s over long portions of it even before Daniel and Fay were born (because she always felt she would have children, and she might be too busy then to remember). Nat's letter was a secret for her eyes only, although now even she had forgotten exactly what the secret entailed, what words of love he had used, exactly, and Daniel, who was ambitious and secretive, had rolled up the letter and stolen it, and taken it home, where his children might see.

"Did you take that picture of the pumpkins and my big letter?" she asked him directly when he came to see her.

"They're safe at my place," he said. "You had everything loose in a box in the garage."

"I knew where it all was!" she objected.

"And now you still know where it all is," he told her.

At the store where he picked up his mail, he'd met the secretary of a famous actress who cured her dog of liver cancer with shark cartilage she got from a woman in New Zealand. Daniel had sent away for the stuff—at his own expense, and why not, if it was legal, since he was a lawyer—and twenty brown bottles arrived by UPS with black eyedroppers in them, but no instructions. The bottles looked to Sura like poison. She kept them in a wicker basket in the den, where she kept the unfinished, unfinishable business of taxes and estate plans, things she thought she might do sometime while she watched the stream of death and terror on TV.

AMONG HER PAPERS she found an old train ticket from New York to Los Angeles. When the war was over, Sura's husband-to-be went ahead to California, where his family lived, to work as a machinist. Sura took the train across the country a month later. She ran away from her mother, from home; that was her biggest adventure, at twenty-two years old. She had a suitcase she'd bought in Times Square and hidden under her desk at her office, a couple of sandwiches and apples she'd taken—her mother would say *stolen*—from home. She had her last paycheck, uncashed, in her purse. She could never go back.

Nat had sent her train ticket together with his extra-large letter. Fortunately, Sura always picked up the mail herself, since her mother worked until six as a seamstress on Fourteenth Street. Sura worked as a secretary for the Christian Record Company—all Christians, but they hired Sura anyway and behaved politely. She felt bad she couldn't give them notice, but her plan had to be top-top secret. The truth was, the largeness of the letter unnerved her. It reminded her of the enormity of the step she was about to take: running away across the country to elope with a man. Her mother would never speak to her again, Sura knew; for the rest of their lives, her evacuation would be a rock at the bottom of both their hearts. Who besides her mother, who had nobody else, nobody in the world, loved her that much?

For three nights, Sura sat up in her coach seat and felt the train pulling her away. On the last night, a soldier bought her dinner in the dining car—a misunderstanding. Sura hadn't mentioned Nat soon enough. The soldier had ordered pork in a cream sauce for both of them, and two bottles of Schlitz beer. Sura had never eaten meat and milk together, and never pork (she'd drunk beer, once). After dinner, he was a little bit forward, and she became sick on the train all the way to Los Angeles, and when she met Nat at Union Station, the city looked pink and yellow under the palm trees, and even Nat looked different and orange. His parents gave her a tiny room of her own overlooking a wall of blue delphiniums, where she lived until she and Nat were safely married.

SURA'S DAUGHTER, Fay, knew a lady who had cured herself. She took a coffee enema every morning and ate nothing but fresh vegetables she ground up in an expensive juicer. She could never eat another dairy product as long as she lived. Fay arranged for Sura to meet this woman on the sidewalk outside Fay's building.

The sun hung low in a silver, smoky sky. Sura climbed awkwardly down Fay's steep steps, wearing a sweatshirt that read I ♥ PRIMATES across the front. Fay wore a baby blue peasant blouse that revealed the murky tattoo above her pubic bone. (What would Fay's future children think of that?) Fay said, "Greta, this is my mother, Sura. Mom, this is my friend Greta."

"It is a pleasure to meet you," Greta said.

"Likewise," said Sura.

Greta had two large dogs on leashes—mastiffs, Fay had warned. She unsnapped the leashes while she talked to Sura and let the dogs run all over the neighbors' lawn. Blond, blue-eyed Greta, it turned out, came from Germany. Sura herself had never stood so close to a German person before. She stood a little closer now than was necessary, as if the health of a woman who had saved herself were an airborne thing, a good germ, or like a hair Greta might shed from her perfect bob, a sacred hair.

Greta wore a black-and-white-checked blazer, a white blouse with button covers striped black and white, and huge, round, black-framed glasses with rose-tinted lenses. In spite of her playful attire, the impression Greta gave off was serious as death. Sura had flung on a wig for this meeting, thank God—her pixie. She felt the sun shining down on her head, and she felt her own new hair growing in underneath the wig, pushing up against the web of another woman's hair.

"So Dr. Santino is treating you?" Sura asked, meaning, of course, Jesus Santino, the famous doctor Fay had found out about—from Greta, obviously.

"Dr. Santino is not *treating you*," Greta said. "You take the regimen and treat yourself. You cure yourself. You totally change your life."

"Change my life?" Sura said.

"You eliminate poisons—dairy, salt, meat."

"Eliminate dairy? My doctor says I need calcium."

"Dairy is poison," Greta told her. "And your doctor says you'll be a skeleton in three months. You want to listen to him?"

"I never had to worry about salt. I have the arteries of a thirteen-year-old."

(Here I am, thought Sura, bargaining with a German woman! A book Fay had given her said bargaining was the first stage of death.)

"This, too, is what your doctor says?"

"Sure," said Sura.

Greta looked up at the sky through her big black rose-tinted glasses and made a screaming sound: "AAAAGH!" Then she said, "Listen, you don't want to cure yourself, don't do it. The regimen isn't for everybody, but I wanted to see my grandchildren grow up, you know? So I go to Dr. Santino. My doctor has killed me off already with his chemotherapy. I've lost fifty pounds and I'm supposed to die in two weeks. So I buy myself a juicer. I eat nothing but vegetable juice I make myself. This is five years ago. I go in once in a while and get my platelets counted, I get a marker. And no cancer! I'm not talking you into anything. I'm just telling my experience. You spend four hours a day in the kitchen, juicing it all up. Every morning, you wake up and you take a coffee enema to purge. This is every morning for the rest of your life."

Sura watched the German woman's enormous dogs dig their claws into the neighbors' turf lawn, which covered the front yard like a green rug.

"Oh my God," she said.

SURA WAS her mother's only child. The way they ate in those days, when food was love! Her mother made latkes and borscht with sour cream, and stewed fruit with more sour cream, not much meat because of the expense, but lots of dairy. Her mother bought cream cheese on a stick (she pulled the money out of her knee-high stockings) and they ate it walking home, just like Popsicles. Her mother poured creamy milk from the bottle into a glass. The milkman came every day to the door. Sura's mother would walk in from work, tie an apron around her waist and start cooking. Two hours she cooked, just for supper. She set one place at the wobble-legged table and watched Sura eat. She never talked, not really, just stray phrases in Yiddish about food and sleep and fabric and fit, because in addition to working in the dress factory and keeping a kosher kitchen, Sura's mother made all their clothes, and took in extra sewing. But there was no single conversation Sura could remember in which they exchanged thoughts or impressions. What her children wanted from her, she couldn't tell them. Sura didn't even know what shtetl her mother had come from in Poland, just that it was in the Bialystok region, taken by the Russians in 1939 and invaded by the Nazis in 1942, when her mother was already on a boat to America.

Then Sura ran away to Nat—he arranged everything—and she never saw or spoke to her mother again, though she wrote to her, of course. When Fay and Daniel asked about her life, about their history, she reached into her mind for happy things to tell them. "We ate cream cheese in the street, just like a Popsicle on a stick," she told them. But they, especially Fay, were never satisfied—they wanted other, more terrible stories.

SURA WENT INSIDE and sat down on the couch, which puffed up cold air. She opened up her book on surviving. Fay moved around the kitchen, making smoothies in the blender. Sura appreciated this gesture for her health, only she wished Fay wouldn't use bananas; they had one hundred calories. When the noise of the blender stopped, Sura read out loud to Fay about a toll-free number in Washington, D.C. "I can send my medical record number to the office of the armed forces. They have state-of-the-art cancer equipment. There is no cost," she called into the kitchen.

Fay came out with a juice glass Sura remembered getting free years ago with a five-dollar purchase at Lucky's. She reached for the glass carefully. All these articles were family history.

"Is that all you got from that book?" Fay asked. "You've been reading the same paragraph for three days."

"It haunts me," Sura said.

"What haunts you?" Fay asked.

Sura's voice rose. "Let me do it my way, that's all!"

She closed her eyes. She remembered certain stories she'd saved and never told her children. One time, her mother took her on a bus trip to the factory where her father worked. It was in another state—Connecticut, Pennsylvania, New Jersey, somewhere like that. They stayed overnight in a boardinghouse. In the morning, they walked to the factory where Sura's father worked and her mother asked for him. After a long time, he came out front, smoking, and right away she started yelling at him in Yiddish for him to come back, to send money. He said in English, "You can't come around here," and sent them away. Sura, pulling on her mother's arm, felt glad. He came home sometimes, though, for a week or a month. When he went away again, the women from the neighborhood would take her mother to have a "hot bath"— that was how you got rid of babies. Her mother grew sick and weak from her "hot baths," yet Sura remembered her working all the time, taking in extra sewing she did at night, cooking with two sets of dishes, everything kosher. She was strong as an ox, and before Sura ran away, she depended on her mother completely.

Why hadn't her mother taken a hot bath to get rid of her? Because she, Sura, was her mother's Love, her Hope.

(Years after her mother died, Sura's father turned up in

California and took two rooms in a not-bad hotel down-town. He brought with him a few old sewing machines, which Sura saw in his room when she and Nat drove down-town to pick him up. They drove him out to the valley for a family supper so the children could meet their grandfather, but she could hardly bear to look at him or speak to him. "How could you be so rude to your own father?" Fay asked her later. "You embarrassed all of us.")

FAY DROVE Sura to Dr. Frank's office in her funny old car.

"Why don't you get an automatic? It's easier," Sura told her. Then she said, "How many earrings have you got in your ears?"

"Nine earrings," Fay said. "Ten holes."

Dr. Frank made them wait. Fay had brought along pic-tures of the trip she and her boyfriend, Ted, had taken to Mexico with another couple. The other woman had long red hair, beautiful hair, almost too much of it, like a wig. Someone—Fay, Sura guessed—had pasted bubbles over the heads in the photographs, which were supposed to show what everybody was thinking. In one picture, the four of them sat at a table around enormous plates of food and bottles of beer. A bubble over Ted's head read "Are we eating again?" In another photograph, Fay stood in front of a pink shack. A bubble over her head read "You see old-world charm—I see a bathroom down the hall."

Fay rattled on about Mexico. Sura waited, listening for

her name. As Fay showed her pictures of hotels, restaurants and pastries, Sura said, "That looks expensive. That looks fattening." Of the countryside, she said, "That looks dirty."

While Fay talked, Sura watched the scrawny woman with baby hair jump up out of her seat and walk to the front desk. She lifted the glass knob of a jar of lollipops, pulled one out, unwrapped it and stuck it into her mouth. Walking past Sura, she winked and, removing the lollipop, held it like a cigarette between two fingers. "What the hell, right?" she said.

Sura shrank back, horrified by this series of gestures, by the way the woman picked her out, winked at her. After Sura's first round of chemo, Fay had told her how beautiful she looked without her wig, how her face looked wise and sculpted. But Fay had also said Sura looked great the year she separated from Nat, those years before he died, when Sura was so independent and went back to school for her A.A. degree.

"You're crazy!" she told Fay. "I didn't sleep for a year! I got those shadows under my eyes that never went away!" She hated it when Fay or Daniel brought up that rough patch. Every marriage had one.

"Why do you bring that up?" Sura had demanded. "Now he's gone, who cares?"

Looking back, it was the years of marriage that counted. Then, ten years ago, Nat had died. He never got to the stage of bargaining. He stayed angry. Fay brought him CDs of the operas he used to like, but he couldn't stand them anymore.

The woman with the lollipop struck up a conversation with the people waiting near her. They all leaned forward, talking at once. Sura felt proud to have her daughter with her in this place; it reflected well to have your adult children care what happened to you. But she found herself tuning out Fay's talk about Chiclets and Incas, actually leaning across Fay's lap a little bit, her ear drawn to these others, even though they weren't talking about selenium and Taxol.

"In kindergarten, I felt I was a special soul," said a man who was very bad off, missing one leg. "My father dragged me in a sled to school. My brother and I shared a pair of mittens to keep our hands warm. I remember warm tears on my cheeks on a snowy day, I loved that girl so much, what was her name, five years old."

"I still think I'm special," the tiny woman with the lollipop said. "You know, God used to talk to me, sit down inside me and say, 'Well, Lila, how are we doing?' That went on until I had my children. I don't blame Him for giving me a little trouble, He knows I can handle it. Or else there's some other reason."

The man in the wheelchair said, "I used to think I was solid all the way through. No organs, no bones. Same on the inside as on the outside. Skin all through. Not so far off—now I got no bones," he said, and they all laughed.

Fay put away her photographs and picked up a magazine. Sura took a pen and a pad from her purse and made a list of things she needed: a new pink bath mat, a bag of spinach, a salad spinner with a cord you pulled, photograph albums for the day she finally got around to putting her pictures in books, which would be harder for her children to steal without her noticing. When the good nurse, Julie, came to the door with her clipboard, Sura stood up automatically, as if, somewhere, a button had been pushed. Fay said, "Why don't you complain, Mom? You let Dr. Frank walk all over you, keeping you here for two hours. You're the *client*." But Sura didn't think of herself as a client; she thought of herself as a *patient*, and anyway, she didn't mind waiting. She waited for Dr. Frank with a kind of attention she couldn't gather at any other time, as if waiting well might bring a reward.

She followed Julie down the narrow hall, past the chemo patients sitting under their bags of cisplatin and Adriamycin, and felt a strange longing to be among them, having chemotherapy together while Dr. Frank worked in his office nearby. Sura had hated chemo, the depression, the anxiety and the sickness, finding herself at Longs as if waking up from a dream with a shoe tree in her cart. After the first time, the count of platelets in her blood fell so low that she needed three transfusions, and she worried to Dr. Frank that she might get AIDS. Dr. Frank said, "Don't worry about AIDS. You've just got cancer, Sura." And now she wanted it; she felt a hunger for the wire in her Broviac, and the antidote and the hydration and the nausea. She wanted to be there, with the other cancer patients doing their protocols together, in the hall.

Dr. Frank told her how well she'd taken the chemo, how determined and strong she'd been. But her white blood count neared zero. Red, too. Shots would bring the counts up, but he knew she wanted the truth. They'd tried everything. The idea had been to give her some time.

"Right!" she assured him. "Time's what I want."

FAY DROVE her home. Sura tried to remember which of her children had had scarlet fever, which one would eat only tuna fish. It was so long ago she was a young mother with a child hanging from her hip, the legs wrapped around her waist. The years she herself had been a child still felt more real than the years she had been a mother. She thought of her mother brushing out her hair at night by the warm stove, and then, more dimly, of herself, brushing Fay's hair. She remembered how, last summer at the Elderhostel, the female ape had leaned into the male, plucking at his hairy shoulders, and how Sophie, the night before she died, had painted her toenails in their dormitory room in Seattle after dinner.

"I want to take that clock I told you about back to Longs, if you've got time," she told Fay.

"I've got time," Fay said—but then she took the clock into the store herself and left Sura in the car. "I know you, you'll lose yourself for an hour," she said.

"Get me one made in America or China, I don't care," Sura told her.

Once Fay had disappeared through the electronic doors, Sura climbed out of the car and walked along the ell of the minimall. The Isle of Wigs was kitty-corner from the

Waxing-Manicure. The Vietnamese women did the best waxing. They had a private room in back where you lay down on a table that was covered with a clean white sheet. One of the women leaned over you and brushed out your eyebrows with a tiny black brush. She put one hand on your ankle, very calm and steady—she had to be. But Sura didn't need those women anymore.

She tugged at the kerchief on her head and released it, stuffed it into her purse. Her leg buzzed beneath her. She felt the sun beating down on her head. It felt good, the hot sun beaming down from the indifferent blue sky.

She opened the door and went inside. The woman behind the counter had on the same baseball cap she'd worn the last time Sura saw her—and the time before that. Across the bill of the cap Sura read the words: I'M OUT OF ESTROGEN—AND I'VE GOT A GUN.

"I know you. You bought the bob," the woman said.

"And the pixie!" Sura told her, hearing the shrillness in her voice. She walked quickly to the rows of Styrofoam heads and stood before them, looking at the chiseled faces, the empty eyes, the white lips, the human hair.

"And now you want something a little more—"

Sura fastened her eyes on the heads. "I don't want anything," she said. "Just looking."

SHE BITES

*T*his man—Froyd—is constructing a postmodern doghouse designed by an architect in Brazil. Froyd doesn't yet own a dog. His role: patronal, advisory. The hired carpenter works in the yard below, laying joists for an outbuilding ten feet wide, twelve feet long and ten feet tall (just small enough not to require a building permit). Plans call for a pine frame sheathed in low-grade plywood and metal siding. The structure will sit thirty feet from the house where Froyd lives with his wife and daughter and a neglected betta fish.

The structure's windows all point west, not to the southeast, where a more energy-aware person would put them. This irritable thought bleeds from the brain of the carpenter, who spent the morning sawing galvanized metal for the doggy door. That job brought small irritations to the surface. The carpenter considers the aesthetic pains the Brazilian architect has taken with the design of this outbuilding/ doghouse a kind of insult against craftsmanship. The dog- house irritates the carpenter on at least two fronts, being both a cheaply built outbuilding and an extravagant doghouse— a willful marriage of bad ideas. The carpenter has long tried to liberate his career from inefficient traditional construc- tion (tarted up in galvanized metal and Plexi) and start his own hay-bale construction business. Working with the noisy, awkward metal sheathing and flashing reminds him that he still lives with his dazzlingly gorgeous blond wife and two blond boys in a thirty-year-old trailer and has been liv- ing this way for the past six years.

Froyd, on the other hand, finds the structure beautiful and modest. Two of the front-facing walls, composed almost entirely of wide sheets of Plexi, offer vistas of the redwoods, which contribute to his property's aesthetic and resale value.

Every half hour or so, Froyd checks the progress of the building by making a pot of coffee for the carpenter and chatting with him for a few minutes—or by looking out the window from his upstairs office. (He has to stand, lean a hand on his desk and crane his neck.) Earlier this morn- ing, Froyd positioned himself for one such look, spilled a jar of pens and cried out in frustration. The carpenter, caught in the act of lighting one of his hand-rolled cigarettes, met Froyd's eye and smiled aggressively.

This tiny shame has not abated yet. It pricks at Froyd. Why should a man apologize for looking at his own doghouse? Even the carpenter (who tried to guilt-trip him into a lugubrious hay-bale "alternative") stands back, looking at the house, judging it. From the tilt of the carpenter's head and from the cigarette smoke billowing around his face, Froyd discerns that the carpenter might be contemptuous, or envious.

Froyd's friend Palmer recommended this carpenter, a favor Froyd appreciated early and regretted immediately, as the unnecessary intimacy of the connection feeds Froyd's paranoid fantasy that the carpenter might mention something to Palmer—something compromising—about Froyd. "He seemed anxious and defensive the whole time," the carpenter might tell Palmer, or "He kept staring at me"—neither of which is true.

While keeping half an eye—a quarter!—on the progress of the doghouse, Froyd prepares a lecture for a course he teaches in the city, a course on forms. In it, Froyd attempts to prove that traditional forms are still the most radical ones. Although he works up his usual heat in arguing this position, Froyd no longer really believes it; he feels contemptuous of the new forms (the constraints and chance patterns) that have replaced the despised forms he knows. In this, Froyd identifies with the hay-bale-loving carpenter, contemptuous of traditional techniques—concrete foundation, floor joists, wall studs, eight-foot ceilings, and suspicious of new architecture. The hay-bale carpenter rages passively against the dumb tradition that proclaims its supremacy over more interesting, more original forms simply by replicating itself again and again—house after house built facing any which way instead of south-southeast, so that a woman reading a book at eleven o'clock in the morning has to burn fossil fuels to make out the words. A similar idea—about forms generally and forms of building in particular—flits like a line of text across the screen of Froyd's mind, and he skims the line as it passes.

Days have passed, and the question remains: Why a doghouse? Froyd needs one, although he doesn't own a dog. He doesn't own a dog for the obvious reason that he doesn't yet have a doghouse. He explained this to the carpenter, who asked. He explained it to his daughter, who asked—repeatedly—for the dog.

When the dog does come, the perfect Plexi sheets will be scratched by the animal's urgent toenails and muddied by paws, breath and drool. Over time, the Plexi will yellow, too—but for now, at this moment, Froyd looks at what he still thinks of as "the doghouse I built for my dog," or "the doghouse I built for my kid," or "the doghouse we put up"—the jocular "we" leaving a generous space around the structure, which is, after all, part of this gift to his wife and his daughter—a doghouse with a dog in it. Every time Froyd looks out the window, though, the harder it is to imagine a dog in the doghouse. Froyd steals another peek at the construction, leaning over his computer, with its cursor blinking over the words "alienated labor, power structures of late capitalism," and cranes his neck until he can see the man to whom he is paying carpenters' wages, whose broad tanned back faces Froyd as he hangs Sheetrock on the walls. What Froyd sees is not a doghouse, but a place of possibilities.

The one possibility Froyd cannot see as he stares through the windows is (frankly) a dog staring back at him, one paw raised dumbly to scratch at the invisible boundary. He considers the porous border between inside and outside, the irrepressible urge to be where one is not. He tries to conjure a dog indistinct enough to be Everydog, and yet particular enough so that Froyd can hear, precisely, the sound of its toe claws on the expensive, fragile plastic.

"WHEN ARE WE GOING to get a dog?" Froyd's daughter asks. She has crept up behind him quietly and caught him peering out at the carpenter. (He should simply have planted himself before the window, his hands behind his back in an attitude of repose, and freely surveyed his creation. "Accept and use your madness," some mad Beat poet once said.)

The top of his daughter's head, he realizes with a touch of horror, comes up to his elbow. Could I have shrunk so far already? he wonders.

Froyd smiles. "It's more complicated than you think."

Froyd's daughter's eyes narrow. "Why is it complicated? I've lived without a dog for nine years. You promised."

Later, she writes Froyd a note and leaves it on the keyboard of his computer, where his lecture waits, rebuking him. "For my birthday I would like a small, brown, medium-size dog. PLEASE do this one thing for me."

Froyd hates the dog already.

MRS. FROYD FINALLY GETS DOWN on all fours, an extension of the yoga she took up in pregnancy, stretching, saluting, elongating, opening. In this position, she feels more in tune with her animal nature. She insists on eating outside. The first time he sees her on the porch, crouching over a bowl, he calls sharply, "Get a spoon!" She has always been critical herself where manners are concerned.

She still dresses every day—good!—and seems cured, too, of the compulsive hand washing. He feels, even, that she could wash *more*—hands and feet. She sleeps with him in the bed.

Froyd does not confide in his friend Palmer. Fear stops him. Instead, he asks, "You know how you fool yourself, thinking a situation will resolve itself? You think you're trying new strategies and they seem to be working?"

"What new strategies have you got?" asks Palmer, himself a desperate man. His wife has a life all apart from Palmer, a spirit world of witchy dust and trickster animals.

"I've got nothing really," Froyd says.

His wife has changed. She pads around barefoot, covered with dirt and mud, and collapses on the white slipcovers. The behavior continues even after he speaks to her reasonably. She just lies under the potted cactus, gnawing on a knucklebone big as her head.

"Do you know how much fat is in one of those?" he asks her. But she simply looks at him with her greeny yellow eyes and chews. Later she skulks off with the bone and comes back with dirt on her nose.

In bed, she licks his face with her tongue as he mounts and thrusts into her. It's the hottest sex they've had in a long time. Afterward, she rolls against him and holds up her stomach to be stroked. Froyd looks at his wife, and his face goes cold. He sits up suddenly. "Get off the bed," he says.

"Off!" he shouts.

She looks at him—stubborn, hurt. He reaches over and pushes her firmly. She tumbles to the floor. She scratches behind one ear, bends impossibly, licks his juices from her hind parts, curls up into a fetal position and sleeps.

The next night, he offers her a cushion beside the bed, but she seems to prefer the doghouse in the backyard. She even uses the doggy door, comes and goes as she likes.

Froyd has spent some time imagining the kind of man he might become if he had a dog—the kind of man who is firm but fair, the kind of man who throws a ball overhand for an hour before dinner. He feels his daughter should take some responsibility; if she can't even take the food bowl to the doghouse in the morning and the evening, and change the water, then—what then?

But children forget. They resent the pet that arrives as a test.

One day, the mother bites her daughter on the hand. (The daughter stuck a pencil in her ear, but still, the behavior crosses a line.) The doctor who puts in the stitches nearly convinces Froyd that she must be put down for it—there can be no excuse for biting a child. But she's rather old already, taking into account the way the years accelerate, and Froyd realizes that he can't bring himself to have his wife shot full of poison at the vet's, or shoot her himself. She is his wife. He still finds her beautiful and desirable. He cannot even condemn her. Benign neglect seems the most humane solution, the simplest thing. He'll wait a reasonable length of time, Froyd figures; then he'll buy his daughter a puppy—a real family dog.

THE ANTIHEROES

*M*onths after our last paycheck, we no longer felt sure we could trust Federico. If he had lied about the first check (in the mail, he'd said, a reasonable argument) and again about the second one, and if he no longer returned telephone calls or e-mails, and kept his shade drawn and his office door locked all day, this did not necessarily reflect on his character.

"Trust me," he'd said on the first day, and we had. After what he had told us about his mother's downfall, how could we not? When Federico was a boy of twelve, in Lisbon, his mother had died before his eyes. She stood at the top of the staircase, a construction of rare Brazilian canarywood, her eyes shining down on him as he waited to hear her speak through the terrible cracking sound of the sky breaking open. Her look expressed embarrassment and a slightly excessive formality, as if she had forgotten his name. "This is strange," she said (in Portuguese); then she died. Her eyes spun out of focus and turned blue (they had always been a dusky green before) and her body rolled headfirst down the stairs. His first instinct was to laugh, Federico said. What could be more absurd than the death of one's mother? It was an impossibility to imagine, he said in that English of his. *Uma intervenção divina—relâmpago* stopped her heart. The loss was *absoluto,* a hole in himself so wide that even grief could not live there, but blew through him violently and rearranged him. He became, at twelve, an *empresário*— a businessman—supporting his father, whose soul had become paralyzed, as well as his sister, a child of eight. The experience turned out not as a *tragédia* but a calling. Give him people on the edge of *catástrofe,* Federico assured us, and he would save them.

Given his qualifications, what could we do but embrace this savior, already hired by unseen and inaccessible forces?

One of us, Boxman, suffered a stroke and could no longer afford the medications he needed to stay alive. The faculty chipped in and bought him a bottle of absinthe. Boxman appreciated the terrible thoughtfulness of the gift. Our health insurance had been summarily canceled; the institute could no longer provide such perks. His former carrier rebilled Boxman for his medical expenses at 800 percent of the original rate—a sum larger than his entire accrued income over a lifetime. Imagine a man's medical bills worth so much more than the man himself! Boxman said. We knew that Federico must appreciate the importance of adequate coverage; just before the cancellation of the health insurance, he'd had a line of polyps removed from his colon. The diagnosis? Not cancer but stress, induced by our situation. Naturally, we sympathized. Our stress infected Federico—contact stress!

Like any great leader, Federico excelled in his early phase, when we knew him only by introduction and projection. It shocked us later to learn that this beach ball of a man, with his pasty skin, his golf shirts, his bald head, his seductive Portuguese accent, was vulnerable, and we began to trust him less.

How could we forget that day, now so many months ago, when the president had brought Federico to us as a last resort? We received him at first with chill hauteur, and Federico said, "What can I do to win your hearts?" Someone said, "Never underestimate the power of an apology." Federico apologized immediately and from his heart for the injustices that had been done to us because of the institute's financial position, which he was already on the point of correcting, well in advance of the final inspection that would decide our fate. He would not disappoint us, Federico promised. *Catástrofe* was his specialty. Not to say that our road would not be hard, but with our help, Federico felt confident that we could recapture the high opinion of the agencies that were about to shut us down.

So we worked harder than ever to correct the messes of the past, to find again the funds borrowed for fact-finding missions to Nicaragua, Iran, Miami and Montreal; to reprint the documents a disgruntled employee had urinated upon; to correct discrepancies and account for unusual services—massage therapy, shock therapy, colonics—the institute claimed to have provided. We worked in the dark in our shadowy stalls (Federico had cut the lights to save electricity). Our mistrust of "the Man" (embodied in the abstract idea of the final inspection) united us. We believed in coalitions, organizing, empowerment, participation, collaboration. Many of us had traveled hard roads before, from Montgomery to Birmingham to Selma, from Cape Town to Cairo. We also felt it important that someone listen to the complaints and threats once the administration began to hide behind locked and shuttered doors. The administration feared for its safety, it said; the students and creditors had grown unreasonable, insane. The police department sent a SWAT specialist, who offered advice on how to handle angry or armed students, and how to behave in a hostage situation: We needed to imagine the institute as a battlefield. Every day, we should visualize and plot our escape route. Whenever we walked into a room, we needed to ask ourselves, "Where would I take cover under fire?" The SWAT specialist taught us to listen for the silence that folowed the discharge of a weapon. "That's the sound you want to hear," the SWAT specialist said.

"Why?" we asked.

"Seize that chance to assault your attacker. Never talk to your attacker, unless you're in a hostage situation. A hostage situation, that's a different story. Don't stand out, but don't be afraid to ask for something—a blanket. You want to be perceived as human."

Those of us with the capacity adapted to the situation.

Most of the students just wanted to transfer. They wanted transcripts, or letters of recommendation, or exculpatory letters for their banks. Federico explained that nothing could be put into writing. The ink on the institute's letterhead had not settled and bled down the page, rendering void any legal communication.

A homeless man took up residence in our office. We found Neville Nevene, the security guard at the school, smoking a blunt in front of the parking lot while reading the collected poems of Arthur Rimbaud. We asked if he could help us escort the man out. Neville did this with uncustomary efficiency, because he hadn't thought of that—he could live in our office. We had a couch; we had a bathroom, a shower, a sink and a coffeepot.

"But the shower doesn't work," we said.

Neville said, "That could be okay."

The board continued to meet at unannounced times in locked rooms, whose windows it covered with a sad assortment of old towels. It did not report on its conversations, its strategies, its decisions. For its own safety (and because of the bleeding letterhead), it put nothing in writing. As weeks and months passed, the board began to detect hostility, even desperation, among the employees at the institute. Hostility and desperation became particulate in the air, like sugar in the atmosphere of a doughnut shop. All the stories began to sound the same, dull rounds of complaints about lost wages and benefits, stories of foreclosure, eviction, the inability to procure life-saving medications, et cetera, as if the board were not already on red alert.

Still, the board took an optimistic view and declined to prepare for the possibility of failure, of institutional collapse. It held its power. It did not respond to questions because it had no answers, and besides, its great power lay in magisterial silence, in the way it sequestered itself in a cold fog of its own. Sometimes we heard, through some wall, the board giggle like a child hiding with its eyes squeezed tight, hysterical with excitement, imagining itself invisible.

Waiting for the board to take action was like waiting for Godot, Neville said. He now lived in our office full-time, carried the collected works of Samuel Beckett under his arm and read out loud part of the famous dialogue between Vladimir and Estragon about how everything depended on Godot, on waiting. He saw everything differently from the rest of us, as if we had all read the same book, but his contained different words, with different meanings. Instead of "Estragon," Neville read "Estrogen" through glasses thick as prisms, slimed with sweat and oil from wiping them on his shirts.

In one thrilling moment, Federico—our savior—launched a coup and seized power. But the disgraced president did not leave. He became a ghost president, wandering the corridor of power—a narrow red-carpeted stretch between his office and the executive toilet. Many of the people who had held positions of power at the institute, even positions of very little power, remained close to the ghost president. Together, they forged a comforting narrative about the historical community of leadership and the principles for which that community stood. What principles? The members of the historical community could not, for practical reasons, put them in writing, but Neville Nevene, who spent an hour a day discussing philosophy with the ghost president in the parking lot, mentioned *structurelessness,* the institute's absolute refusal to tidy up its humanity to please the Man—the Man being the creditors, the final inspectors, the whole capitalist-military-industrial complex, and most of the faculty, including the activists and the union and the women of color, and the women in general, and the men of color, and the gender queers.

But, we asked (through our emissary Neville), didn't our continuing presence at the institute prove our commitment to enlightenment, justice, a politics of meaning, a community of soul? Not really, the board shot back. The historical community functioned like a family.

Yes, we agreed. The institute was patriarchal and arbitrary, and we loved it for the same reasons people love a family: because we felt connected to it, and believed that in some imperfect and provisional way it loved us back, tolerated us and demanded our loyalty.

*　　*　　*

WAS THAT the ghost president standing alone on the street corner, talking into a toy cell phone?

Was that the ghost president standing alone outside of the oxygen bar, playing an accordion?

FEDERICO NO LONGER looked us in the eye when we met in (or near) the corridor of power. We waited in the shadows for him to emerge from the executive toilet. We held out scraps of paper for him to sign, excuses and apologies we ourselves lacked the authority to make. Occasionally while we waited, we saw the accountant, a shadow of her formerly robust self, moving quickly along the wall. When she saw us, she would shout in her heavily accented English, "Let me out! Let me out! I am kept against my will!" But the longer we waited in the corridor for Federico to come out of the executive toilet, our miserable scraps of paper damp in our hands, the more we pretended not to notice her Mandarin oaths and mutterings. The accountant had once produced charts and budgets, and we felt, still, that we needed her.

After the authorities contacted us regarding our missing pay, Federico refused to sign our slips of paper or acknowledge us. We would, individually, be held responsible for scheduled income, the authorities promised. No use trying to evade or equivocate. No paperwork had been filed on our behalf; they had our number; we would pay as scheduled, or they would throw us in jail! So we continued to work; even Federico, who had not been paid himself, continued.

In this way, we traveled beyond the realm of the heroic, and became contemptible to one another and to ourselves. We had no wages, no benefits; some of us had even grown sick and died. We were complicit in our oppression; we knew that. The conditions felt sickeningly familiar to some of us who had survived other experiences of humiliation. Yet we continued to show up.

It became difficult to know whether our presence helped or hurt. At the first cracking sounds, the ghost president and Federico cautiously opened the door to the executive toilet, where they now hid together. Because of the narrowness of the toilet, the ghost president could not see past the beach-ball form of Federico. "*É um milagre,*" Federico told him—a miracle—as the whole building began to rattle like dice.

The cracks widened. We mounted the beautiful walnut staircase collectively, and used simple tools—hammers, Phillips heads.

OUR OLD COLLEAGUE O'Malley had always sung variations on one note: He represented an oppressed and colonized minority. O'Malley had worked as a Teamster, a merchant seaman. Colcannon and ale ran in his blood; he fought in and stewarded some union that did not apply to us. His face looked like fire and brimstone and he loved nothing more than the clarity of an enemy.

He fixed on Irene because, as part of the historical community, O'Malley still defended the ghost president. Besides, he said, Irene was bourgeois—all the activists were bourgeois, not fighting for real things, such as living conditions, wages, and so on, but, rather, for luxuries, such as sexual freedom. But Irene had been in a union, too, up in Canada. She'd seen how sexist it was, how dominated by men, like everything in Canada was dominated by men—by bluenecks and blockheads and by the oppressive cold and by old fucked paradigms. O'Malley took exception to Irene's characterizing the union as sexist and accusing him of being an old fucked paradigm, turning him into a stereotype because of his working-class accent. He knew this game, he said. He held his fists balled in his lap, as if he were trying to keep himself from leaping up and clocking Irene. "I won't have my people slandered and reduced to cheap stereotypes," O'Malley shouted, "the great working class who invented the lively language of slang, on whose backs this nation was built, by a bunch of old dyke Canucks."

Irene rose to her full height—six foot three—and bent over O'Malley until he disappeared. In this way, sadly, we began to dispatch one another.

EVERY DAY, a new message came from someone: "I'm sorry, I can't stay anymore," listing debased conditions—a litany of apologies. One could no longer afford a bus pass; another couldn't keep up her strength without her AIDS medication; another had moved in with his mother, who insisted that he be home every night at five-thirty. One couple, known throughout the institute as bon vivants, invited us over for a farewell dinner. They were in the process of losing everything—electricity, gas, heat, car, apartment. They still had a bidet, though. We ate Cuban beans with a ham hock and drank a few bottles of Margaux they'd saved for twenty years for a special occasion—the occasion now being the end of an era of wine and roses, collaboration and solidarity! We pitied our lost colleagues, and, yes, we feared them. After that rich evening, we never saw them again.

SWING

*D*uring the season Riva thought of as the autumn of her divorce, life became so quiet that she heard fog drip. Big spongy porcini pushed up under the orange pine needles and hissed as they grew, distracting her from the uninhibited exposé of the county school board she'd tried for weeks to write on assignment from the socialist weekly, whose primary agenda—"to fan the flames of discontent"—was broadcast on the masthead. As she worked, Riva thought about butter and shallots sizzling in the pan and the way she and Roberto used to laugh before dinner, their glasses of red wine on the scarred wooden table, some Ghanaian highlife CD playing on the stereo. She thought about the atmosphere she and Roberto made together those five years, about mushrooms and butter and wine and bare feet and West African music, as if happiness were a country where she'd once owned a house. Without Roberto, she didn't even bother to open a bottle of wine (she'd only drink it all), and she ate cold, hard food: apples from the tree, carrots from the garden, crackers from the general store. She drank water from the well. Brutal simplicity felt weirdly comforting. Sometimes she woke in the night, rattled by a ringing, dinning silence so profound, she might have been at the center of deep space.

What she missed most were barefoot nights, dancing on the beach around a fire, or on the floor of the movie theater when live bands came and the house manager took out the first two rows of seats. She missed tipping her dirty feet back into high heels at midnight and riding home next to Roberto in the blue Taurus. She missed his greatness of spirit, his exuberant ways, the intoxicated poetry that surrounded those moments of terror and pleasure in the car. "Uncork the night!" he'd shouted out the windows, driving fast and confidently down the coast road while she gripped the wheel. "Breast against the triumphant curve and fly down the dirt road unbuckled, casting sparks!"

In retrospect, she could see how codependent she had been.

SHE'D LEFT Roberto because he hit her; it hurt to say this so simply. He'd hit her more than once—twice, or three times, jarring smashes of knuckles in her face. That she didn't, at thirty-four, remember the apparent provocations or the number of hits worried her most of all. Forgetting, diminishing, or rationalizing violence made *her* complicit, guilty! Roberto, too, implied that Riva shared a dynamic role in the hitting, which he called "arguing."

"It takes two to tango," he'd said once.

The first time he hit her instantly created a rift so deep, she knew she must leave him. Within five minutes of his first swing, they were undressed, fucking. Riva's black eye bloomed under Roberto's caresses. His tenderness, as he touched her, made her shiver. She put his fingers on the wound again and again, definitely the wrong message to send.

The blue-and-yellow swelling dropped down her face over the course of four days, until she looked like a gerbil. While her eye and cheek healed, Roberto picked up the mail and ran errands. Riva appreciated his kindness and discretion. She worked at home anyway, mostly. She did most of her interviews by telephone or e-mail, more than a first-rate reporter would, because even without livid marks, she was shy.

Roberto also worked from home. He had a framing business, made artisan frames from old-growth redwood and salvaged metal. Sometimes he made garden beds, a similar process: He made frames for art and frames for dirt. His frames were the real thing, everyone agreed, more artful and interesting than 99 percent of the work they enclosed. Roberto was famous for his frames, and for his raised beds, which framed the earth, and famous for the weed he grew in the woods just over their property line, his macho, big-budded sensimilla, not organic but very strong. He sold to artists in the city, to people Riva and Roberto counted as friends, although in the end the friendships grew strained and broke. Roberto was Riva's best friend, and because by most people's standards Roberto's personality veered toward the eccentric and difficult, their friendships with others had been abraded (by Roberto's abrasiveness) and eroded. Inviting people in became awkward. The house smelled skunky: Sometimes Roberto washed money and hung it up to dry on a clothesline in the bathroom. Neither Riva nor Roberto possessed a traditional moral compass, she knew that, but toward the end she did not like to have people see the way she and Roberto lived. They might see things about Roberto and the shape of their life together that she could not see herself.

She still loved him completely; she loved most his rough, edgy side. Even after he hit her, his presence held a chemical charge.

Roberto moved out when she asked. He didn't seem surprised. He wept; he packed his things in a Hefty bag. He backed up his flatbed to his framing studio, laid all his wood, scrap metal and tools in the back and drove away. He moved into a trailer up on the ridge, an awful situation, she imagined, a real comedown from the beautiful life the two of them had made together. Then she saw him in town at a harvest party with a very young woman who looked like a teenager, sexed and clueless. Poor Roberto, Riva thought. How sad. But Roberto didn't look sad. He looked happy, dancing with the teenager on the pier. Her long blond hair kept blowing into his eyes. The teenager looked happy, too. Roberto looked as beautiful as she remembered, his ravaged, tragic face bathed in light from the moon and the bonfire, his eyes lit by drink. The poor girl, Riva thought, imagining the end of the evening in Roberto's depressing trailer. He will hit her, too, she thought. Maybe not tonight—but he will. The thought gave her a thrill of Schadenfreude, which made her immediately ashamed of herself, and proud that she had left him.

At the party, she also saw—and successfully avoided—a neighbor whose pit bull had twice attacked her dog, Spinoza, dug its teeth deep into Spinoza's haunch, causing trauma and a big medical bill. When she called the neighbor the first time, he apologized. When she called after the second incident, he said, "You know, this never happened before, and now it's happened twice with you. What's your dog doing to provoke my dog? Is it a female?" Riva protested, but the neighbor just talked over her. "Sure, I could tie my dog up, but nothing's more sorrowful than a tied-up dog. So I'm just not going to do it. If my dog attacks your dog again, take some personal responsibility—just shoot it. Put it out of your misery."

She lived among maniacs! Of course Riva would not shoot her neighbor's dog. Roberto used to keep a gopher rifle in the house, but Riva couldn't stand it, and he finally gave it away. So she didn't even own a gun.

At the harvest party, she avoided Roberto and the neighbor, as well as the kind of mountain men—the growers, the hermits, the felons—who preyed on single women like herself. Instead, she chatted with a woman named Aisha, who had been with Riva and Spinoza in puppy-training class. Aisha had stopped going because her puppy—an enormous Great Dane—had choked to death on a treat at the beginning of the third class.

"I'm doing great," Aisha said. "Byron and I take tango. It's changed our life. We're both in amazing shape, our sex life is hotter, and I see him again as a human. You should come—bring Roberto."

"Roberto and I separated," Riva said.

"Oh—well, then you should come find somebody."

Riva thought of Roberto saying, "It takes two to tango" with a soupçon of bitterness, and then she didn't think more about it. A few days later, she found a flyer in the coffeehouse. Not tango, but a swing class in a town an hour to the north where the partners—and Riva—would be new.

SHE'D DEMANDED from Roberto custody of their terrier mutt, Spinoza, and he had quickly agreed, seeing all her logic. But then Spinoza died, killed by a raccoon that took to hanging about the place after Roberto left, even going so far as to sit and wait by the front door for food, as Spinoza himself had always done. After the horrific cleanup and burial of her pet, Riva felt shaken, anemic, as if she'd lost blood. She tried to call Roberto to break the news, but the phone rang and rang; Roberto's alienation ran so deep, he didn't even have a machine.

After Riva went to bed, stimulated, weeping and exhausted, the raccoon came into the house—it turned the knob on the door. She ran to greet the intruder, which she mistook for Roberto, thinking he'd come back. The raccoon stood at the bowl of compost with its paws open, the pads lined like human palms (it had a fate!), its fat digits like Russian banana potatoes, its nails mandarin, tobacco-colored. The empty wine bottle lay on the floor, as if flung there in disgust, with mud prints across the label.

"Hey," Riva cried. "Hey, hey, *hey, hey!*"

The raccoon turned, still chewing, twenty pounds of greed and insolence, and faced her.

"You," Riva screamed. "You, you, you, you, you!" She switched on the lights. The raccoon kept its eyes on her and backed toward the door, three-legged, its spine arched. Riva growled out a threat and rushed forward suddenly. The animal picked up an apple from the floor, then stood up to its full height and threw it at Riva. She ducked; the apple knocked her elbow and rolled harmlessly away, and as the raccoon backed outside, it gave her a knowing look. She cried in bed later, loud wailing sobs the raccoon could probably hear.

NOW STORMS ROLLED IN off the Pacific like wet gray walls closing in. Water poured from the milky sky and turned the fields and ferns a lusher green. The calla lilies near the front door grew as big as oil funnels and the bark on the redwoods took on a more lively form, like the hide of an animal. Riva found an old grass bag in the back of her closet, its surface covered in a mold that looked exactly like rabbit fur. She burned it in the woodstove. The woodpile outside swelled with damp under its blue tarp and she burned anything expendable. The indoor air turned heavy and smoky, though with a bright tang of pine.

She worked on a story for the socialist weekly about a logger who'd come up from Jalisco, Mexico, to labor as a choker setter. A mountain of talus spilled down on top of him during a job—the timber company had tagged some old-growth trees on a steep slope above the river—and killed him. Environmentalists argued that those trees were protected by previous agreements, that the choker setter didn't even speak English, that the timber company had not properly apprised the worker of the danger. Riva's job: to get the real scoop, make the family and the loggers talk, get the foreman to talk, take the usual disorganization of points of view and tell a story that didn't want to be told. A story emerged like a landscape; it didn't exist until somebody put a frame around something and said, *Look here.*

Meanwhile, the foreman who filed the accident report (which became the death report), said, no story here, only an act of God. The environmentalists talked, but they demanded that the story conform to certain moral truths that the story did not exactly conform to. The choker setter's family talked a little, in Spanish, and revealed nothing. They'd been paid off—"In dollars?" Riva asked in her debased high school Spanish—in exchange for their silence. They also feared exposure of their relatives, one of whom, Riva learned, came across at Juárez in the bed of a truck loaded with carrots. The mainstream newspaper tried to redirect the conversation, and ran a two-page spread in the newspaper about the honorable history of logging across generations, emphasizing the life-and-death nature of the work, the shrewd and solitary nature of the logger. Never mind that the choker setter had been an untrained illegal twenty-three-year-old immigrant working for minimum wage who understood so imperfectly the danger of his occupation that he'd hidden behind a tree when the mountainside gave way. Riva had to clear away enough of the words so people could understand what kept happening. "Just get the moral truth," the editor told her. "Those bastards—they're all bastards. That's the story."

Both sides told the story the same way, with the choker setter as a victim. One side called him a victim of corporate greed; the other side called him a victim of nature, or of an act of God. The choker setter, an invisible man named Jesus Cruz, didn't have a side. There didn't seem to be a way for his story to extend beyond the frame already nailed down around it. The story took place around Jesus, outside of his story. The story itself depended on who told it. Riva suddenly felt filled with energy, inspiration and insight— a form of rage. The victim must become the subject of his own story; he must be seen. Riva let them all have it—the timber company, the environmentalists, the newspapers that covered the story as one about courage or honor or corporate greed. They were all bastards, just as the editor had said, but she felt that she had finally come to this conclusion on her own evidence, honestly. She wrote for twelve hours, and when she finished, she felt tired, clean and conscious of a ravenous hunger, a gnawing so vivid, it was less like lust and more like a bacterial infection. She found a steak in the freezer, seared it on the stove and ate it, still frozen in the middle, while drinking a whole bottle of red wine. This was the meal that Edward Abbey ate to steel himself in the wilderness to greet a bear. As she ate, Riva steeled herself, and dug out the telephone number she'd written down for the swing class.

The dances took place on Friday nights in the beautifully named town of Madrigal, at the Community House. You could drink artisan gin from a still in the Anderson Valley; you could drink organic hard cider from a farm. Riva had to drive home after, and she didn't want to take a chance on being pulled over. The police would take her an hour and a half to the county seat, she'd have to spend the night in jail, and then they'd have her license. She didn't even know how she'd get home if that happened. Her name would appear in the police blotter. Plenty of nights she and Roberto had stepped out for the evening, gone to bars or parties, and he drove home. (Once, she'd reached over from the passenger side and actually steered the car for a few minutes while he pressed the gas and sang "Spirit in the Dark" exactly as Aretha sang it.) What a pliant idiot she had been! She'd always taken care to drink very little when out with Roberto, so that if a deputy pulled him over and hauled him to jail, she could post bail and drive them home. She'd always kept a check in the glove compartment of the Taurus, just in case.

THE SWING CLASS DREW more women than men. Riva got the last one, a tall, well-built person named Norman who lived in the woods outside of Madrigal and looked as fit as if he climbed trees all day—which he did, as it turned out. He'd had a girlfriend, but she couldn't take the winter and the rain, he said. She'd moved back to the city; he liked it here.

The instructors demonstrated a few steps and let the class loose. Norman danced terrifically, sensually, philosophically. They traded partners, then always came back to each other. Riva loved the homey feel of the Community House, which smelled of sweat and venison, and the slippery lyrics that spilled from the speakers: "Satin Doll," "A String of Pearls," "I Can't Give You Anything but Love."

"Dancing is a conversation, an improvisation," Norman told her. "You take in a bit of me and give back a bit of you. Nothing you say in words touches the truth of what you say through the ends of your fingers." He touched the ends of her fingers to his, and she instantly saw what he meant. She could follow him perfectly. Then he pulled his fingers away and communicated through vibrations in the air between them. He did it simply by looking into her eyes.

Soon Riva was swinging across the floor, her body graceful and knowing. She drank a little of the artisan gin, and felt suddenly that the center of her story lay in the standpoint of the blue pumps she wore. She kicked them off and they leaned into each other like a blue couple watching from the sidelines.

During the break, Riva sat with Norman on a couch in back. He asked her serious questions and they fooled around under a gray blanket. She had never talked to a stranger this way before. "I wish I had a formal, spiritual life," she told him, "somebody else's structure. Sometimes I fast for Yom Kippur, but I never feel much except hungry."

Whatever Riva had felt so intensely in the vibrations in the air between them intensified under the blanket, where their parts touched in several places. "The spiritual condition of hunger works as well as any religion," said Norman, his eyes and fingers twinkling. "It might even be the point of fasting."

"You're still a beautiful woman. You have a hot body," Norman said. Riva felt a wet object penetrate her ear: his tongue, which functioned exactly like a knife through her heart.

"You do something to me," he sang, which made her feel, dangerously, like an instigator. Someone began clapping and the room throbbed. Norman danced Riva through the doorway, onto the porch and across the lawn.

"Go Norman," someone said.

The rain had stopped and stars at unimaginable distances from one another—light-years—blazed together. Riva sat behind Norman on his motorcycle, her bare feet resting on cold metal rods. He spun out of the gravel parking lot and drove straight through the three stop signs in town before cutting loose onto the highway. Her arms tightened around his ribs. Squeezing hard, she opened the throttle to the sweet familiar surge. The tighter she held him, the faster he went.

OPAL IS EVIDENCE

*I*n a state of mindful trepidation, Jude brought her friend Trina to her house-sit at the Goldsteins' yurt. Trina would help out during Jude's daughter's recovery from surgery and give moral support, since Opal's recovery was expected to be temporary, really part of an overall decline. On the ride from Oakland to Panther Point, Opal slept in her infant car seat between Jude and Trina. The car seat still fit, sort of, even though Opal was nearly ten; it cradled her small body while she slept. Opal was still not entirely *here,* Jude reminded herself when Trina passed a doobie across Opal's body. The tissue around her brain still ebbed and swelled, the hospital's plastic diaper crackled under her nightgown, and a bandage bound her head. Yet—how Opaline—she wore pink lipstick and a dangling bead earring. A felt bag Jude had run up on her sewing machine hung from Opal's round wrist, filled with jelly beans Opal had tried (and failed) to count in the hospital. Jude looked away from Opal while she blew smoke out the window. When they got to the Goldsteins', Jude lifted her limp daughter from the car seat. Opal shouted, "My purse! My purse!" without really waking up. Her hands beat against Jude, found the jelly bean purse, then settled.

As Jude carried her across the threshold, Opal opened her eyes and said, "What's this?"

"We're staying at the Goldsteins' yurt, babe," Jude told her. "It's round."

"Cool," said Opal.

The Goldsteins' yurt, in fact, formed a hexagon (a level of detail beyond Opal at the moment), with a pickle barrel attached to one wall. It *was* cool. At the apex of the dome, a window like a lens peered up at the sky, or zoomed in, like a microscope. Even in the main space of the yurt, you could feel the efflorescence of the grow room downstairs, where the plants sprang up lush under lavender grow lights, ripe-smelling, skunky and green.

Jude's job: to house-sit for a month while the Goldsteins laundered their marijuana money in Hawaii. Coals to Newcastle, Jude told them, but they didn't know what she was talking about. Jude hailed from back east, from a farm in Pennsylvania, where the references were different.

Trina had promised to help with Opal, whatever Jude needed. But once in the yurt, comfort overwhelmed her and she behaved like a guest. Jude made pancakes; dishes piled up. For their third night together, Jude defrosted one of the Goldsteins' free-range chickens and organized a dinner party, a celebration of Opal's return from the hospital and ritual removal of her head bandage.

Jude's friend Egon arrived at six—he'd gotten a ride from some friends who planned to wait for him in the parking lot at the pier. "Why don't you invite your friends to join us?" Jude asked sincerely. She suddenly felt the need of more celebrants, more company, but Egon seemed to know better.

Opal dressed in the pickle barrel, where Jude had set out clothes and stuffed animals. Jude put the chicken in the oven to roast and made a salad, using the Goldsteins' mahogany salad bowl and tongs, and lettuces from their garden. Trina and Egon talked about where they'd come from. Egon had lived in Bolinas, then Germany, then here. Trina had built up camps all over the Midwest and the West, but mostly she had been run out of campgrounds.

"My camps were burned to the ground," Trina said. "I was run out of Bellingham, Christopher, Curtis, Marcus, Ronald and Lyle, Washington, as a witch. Run out of Donald and Eugene, Oregon. Everywhere I went—ostracized. I built up a beautiful compound, with tepees and healings. A beautiful place."

"Where did you build up the compound?" Egon asked.

"In every place," said Trina.

"That's too bad."

Trina shrugged. "Good comes from bad—that's my religion. It's karmic science."

"What religion is this?" Egon asked.

"True religion," Trina said. "It's Buddhist-Wiccan-theosophy. Have you heard of Sufi Nigiri?"

Egon shook his head. "I never heard of it."

OPAL EMERGED from the pickle barrel wearing a wedding dress—a bristling garment of tea-colored lace. It dribbled down over her feet on the rug. Jude put her hand over her mouth when she saw Opal and her eyes filled with tears. "You look gorgeous, babe," she said.

"I know," said Opal.

They sat on the rug, an enviable Persian kilim. The efflo-rescence of the grow room produced an atmosphere that adhered to the inside of Jude's nose. In spite of herself, she mapped out venues where she could unload a few ounces. To calm her monkey mind, Jude organized the altar: a candle, an abalone shell, a sage smudge stick, a feather, a cloth snake filled with buckwheat hulls. Opal sat cross-legged in front of Jude while Jude cut through the head bandage, removed it from Opal's head and laid it—stained with blood and pus—in the center of the altar.

Let them see it! Jude had seen it. Opal had worn it. Not an ordinary American life, but her life, and Opal's life—let America see. Jude lit the sage with a Bic lighter and cleaned herself with the smoke, drawing it around her head and down the outline of her body—her shoulders, waist and legs, around her feet. She smudged herself—story of her life—then she smudged Opal in the candlelight. The atmosphere here so different from the hospital, where white lights had burned beside Opal's hospital bed, parked next to the nurses' station. (Jude stayed there, too, of course, almost every minute, crawling into the bed next to Opal for an hour now and then to fall into an instant sleep in which she dreamed that she was awake, sitting on Opal's bed in the hospital, next to the nurses' station.) Here at the Goldsteins', though, Jude controlled the atmosphere. She handed the sage to Egon, who smudged Trina. Trina smudged Egon, who handed the smudge stick to Jude.

Jude handed the bird feather to Opal. "You speak first," she said. Opal took the feather, gathered up the skirts of the wedding dress and said, "This is a ceremony for my brain tumor. I have had an operation to take the tumor, but now it is growing back over my speech and hearing. This is why I have called you all here."

She looked at Jude, who said, "Go ahead and sing a little song, Ope." Opal sang:

> *Help me help me spirits go away*
> *Help me help me spirits go away*
> *My brain tumor is growing*
> *But I want to stay.*

She stopped and stared upward, through the lens of the yurt, then lowered her eyes and handed the feather to Trina.

"Perfect, beautiful," said Trina.

"I know," said Opal.

Trina held the feather and crossed her arms over her chest. She bowed her head and waited so long in such stillness, Jude wondered if she'd gone to sleep. Finally, instead of speaking, she made a gargling sound and sucked moisture up into her nose.

"Who are you?" Opal asked.

"Your next-door neighbor on the boat," Trina said, wiping her eyes.

Jude smiled at Trina. "She knew you as a man," she said.

"I don't remember him at all," Opal said.

Trina pulled a handkerchief from her fanny pack and blew her nose. She thought some more and then said, "Precious Opal, precious, precious jewel, I talked to the Great Spirit and she said this tumor is not part of you. She said to open your mind to healing, and the light of love and health will shine in and the cancer will fizzle like a pizzle."

"What's a pizzle?" Opal asked.

"Bull's willy," said Jude.

Opal stood up. "Mom, can I take off this dress?"

"Sure you can," said Jude.

Opal pulled the dress over her head. Underneath she wore a white nightgown and cowboy boots.

Trina handed the feather to Egon, who said, "Wow, I'm blown. I am blown away," and handed the feather to Jude.

Jude said, "Apple juice, cell phones, aluminum cookware, fluoridated water, formaldehyde carpets, lead toys, lead fish. My father still smokes, his farm a poison swamp. Opal poisoned before she was conceived. What more evidence do we need? Opal is evidence. But who do I kill? You know what I mean? America?"

Trina nodded, and said, "I've been run out of half the small towns in America because I profess the true religion. How sick is that?"

Jude bent over her buck knife and began cutting Opal's head bandage into strips so everyone could burn some. "We'll use the woodstove—we'll definitely be fire-safe this time!" she said.

"I'd like to sing another song," Opal said. Her arms waved like wands in the air and she sang:

My tumor grows bigger in my brain.
But here in this round room
People pray
For me here with my tumor
Growing in my brain.

Trina wiped her eyes with the backs of her hands. Egon played "Kumbaya" on an acoustic guitar, and Opal sang along in a sweet, high voice. Jude lit the fire, which hissed and popped in the woodstove.

Trina picked up the wedding dress from the floor and laid it tenderly over a chair. "How do you save all this stuff?" she asked Jude. "The whole time I've known you, you've lived on a boat or a bus."

Jude shrugged. "This was my mother's wedding dress," she said. "Those were my cowboy boots when I was nine years old." She laughed. "It's all my legacy," she said. "I had every Barbie doll, too, but my sister sold them on eBay. I have my grandmother's photograph album of scary Scandinavians. I have her china cupboard filled with a dinner service for twelve. It's lived everywhere I lived because I thought there would be a future. Who knows? Maybe."

Jude's jaw clenched. She felt the furious solitude of her fate—to fight for the weak and expose the guilty. It was the sap in her veins that kept her body upright.

Opal sang:

America, America, God shed her grace on me!
And crown her good with brotherhood
From sea to shining sea!

Jude handed out pieces of the head bandage to Opal, Trina and Egon. One by one, the four of them threw their bandages into the woodstove. The strips of gauze blackened and melted together into a viscous, hard helmet, which smoldered on, even hours later, when they ate.

AMONG THE MEZIMA-WA

*M*y son, Sam, spent a year on a fellowship doing advanced work on the culture and civilization of the Mezima-Wa. When he came home for the summer, he brought a Mezima-Wa woman with him. Natalie was not a traditional Mezima-Wa; in fact, she'd grown up in St. Louis, where she attended the Burroughs School on a merit scholarship before matriculating at Villanova and taking the Mezima-Wa option for her junior year abroad. A year among the Mezima-Wa had irrevocably changed both my son and Natalie, they agreed. They were blown away by the culture, the colonial legacy, the horror, the architecture, the tribal music and the tribal language (Mezima-Wa). They came back earnest and politicized, decrying the effects of U.S.-backed "economic development" projects that supposedly raised the standard of living of the Mezima-Wa but commodified the forests and shorefront, on which the entire culture depended. I roasted a chicken and made a pilaf, and as we sipped *vin ordinaire,* I asked about their experiences among the Mezima-Wa; I asked for pictures. But they couldn't tell me anything, because I had not been there; it was as if the year among the Mezima-Wa had cleaved them away from common life and made us (parent, offspring, girlfriend of offspring) strangers to one another. Of course, Natalie *was* a stranger. I know nothing of the customs of the Mezima-Wa, nor even those of young American women from back east.

In those first weeks in July, during which they kept erratic hours—not to impugn Mezima-Wa hours—Natalie and Sam tried to be patient. In short: When I woke, they slept, curled together in Sam's childhood twin bed; if I brushed my teeth and put on pajamas, they spontaneously decided to make a feast of Mezima-Wa foods from the hill country. This required a ritual bathing of their feet in the bathtub, followed by a cleansing of the tub with my good balsamic vinegar and hideous bathroom sponge. They then filled the floor of the tub with the tough leafy vegetables, dampened grains and fish, which, along with a tuber called *chloc,* form the basis of Mezima-Wa cuisine. (Sam and Natalie substituted frozen hake for the usual stockfish and jicama for the *chloc.*) They pounded and stomped the mixture with their clean feet, forming the solids into neat balls by manipulating their toes and rubbing their soles together.

Seeing the two of them sitting shoulder-to-shoulder on

the edge of the tub in their bright-colored tunics and cutoff jeans reminded me of what Roland Barthes called "the fabulous comforts" of domestic life. Since my ex-husband Bob's defection from marriage and from America, prompted by certain impetuous but unoriginal actions on my part, life had devolved into tidiness and convenience. Natalie and Sam, ankle-deep in their bathtub stew, reminded me of my own erotic history and, by extension, the whole human history of messy pleasures.

Sometime after midnight, they poached the fish balls in my wok (the Mezima-Wa drop them into clay vats of oily broth, where they rise like matzo balls) and used the liquids (traditionally scraped from the mashing tub with a freshwater shell) as the base for fiery sauces. Natalie produced endless spice packs, which she kept not in the kitchen with the other spices, but in her own purse.

This was not to be ungenerous, she assured me—generosity was the highest value among the Mezima-Wa—only for safety: Mezima-Wa spices were mildly psychotropic and could cause seizures in any but the smallest doses. Each was absolutely essential to the authenticity of the dishes.

They fed the fish balls—*boibois*—to each other in the Mezima-Wa way, reclining on my off-white sofa near dawn, their fingers in each other's mouths. My pleasure in their company was diminished somewhat by perimenopausal symptoms—sporadic irritability, trouble sleeping, numbness, a new rigidity in my shoulders and spine. (Dr.

Berman had suggested homeopathic doses of bioidentical estrogen and a pinch of testosterone—good for the libido, she said.)

Sometimes I rose to the demands of maternal generosity and offered to make a Western breakfast when Sam and Natalie awoke at one or two o'clock in the afternoon. Natalie would whisper into Sam's ear at such length and with such urgency that I thought she must be revealing some secret. My first thoughts ran to pregnancy, a thrill and a panic—what beautiful, brilliant children they could make!—until finally Sam nodded and said, "Natalie would like two eggs over easy with some ham and, if you have them, a few sardines. Canned are fine. I'll just have Grape-Nuts, thanks."

While among the Mezima-Wa, Sam had sent regular texts from his cell phone—a form suited to his terse, epigrammatic style. From these communiqués, I'd gathered that Natalie's year abroad had not pleased her parents, who actually stopped speaking to her for several months. Part of the trouble seemed to be cultural; having so recently left the region themselves for the economic opportunities they hoped a life in America would make possible for their daughter, they objected to her return to the nation-peninsula (engaged in a civil war when they left, which Natalie barely remembered) and to her study of the Mezima-Wa culture as a living, dynamic possibility. It seemed to them that they had the best of both worlds in St. Louis—Mezima-Wa values within an American economy and a capitalist structure that protected their investments, including and especially Natalie.

After Villanova, they expected Natalie to attend Harvard Medical School and become, like her aunt, a pediatrician.

Maybe, too, Natalie's return to the Mezima-Wa struck them as romantic or frivolous. "Bet they grieve loss of their homeland," I'd texted Sam.

"Grief counselor examines world through lens of sorrow," he'd texted back.

What other lens could I use? Four mornings and two afternoons a week, grief knocked at my office door, presented evidence (lost children, failed marriages, demented parents, financial ruin, existential dread). This is not to say that I don't love my job; grief counseling is the most satisfying work I have ever done—it brings me pleasure, and I believe in the process. Twenty years of compelling narratives have convinced me that as an organizing principle for life, grief works.

DURING THE COURSE of their daughter's year abroad, Natalie's parents came to understand and accept that Sam was not a traditional Mezima-Wa man. (The initial confusion stemmed from Sam's name, which is actually the Mezima-Wa word for "calabash" or "capacious urn"—an auspicious symbol.) They realized that in returning to Mezima-Wa, Natalie wasn't unraveling all their work in coming to the United States, but, rather, reclaiming her identity and cultural heritage as a Mezima-Wa while maintaining a friendly, nonsexual relationship with a promising and affluent(!) American-born boy. On the other hand, when they learned that Sam wasn't Mezima-Wa-American, but just a random person Natalie had met during her year abroad, and with whom she lived in unseemly proximity, they naturally began to worry that Sam might not fully appreciate the urgent, paramount importance of Natalie's remaining a virgin until her wedding day. Their concern eventually reached a hysterical pitch.

Then came the bombshell, a text from Sam: "Natalie and I plan to marry on return to States. Yes we're sure." Sam assured me that Natalie's parents were relieved and had expressed willingness to accept Sam as a husband (according to Mezima-Wa tradition, he would be called "Husband" not only by Natalie but also by her parents). They had also accepted me as the husbandmother.

Natalie's parents arrived at the beginning of July at my house in Santa Cruz for the monthlong visit that precedes any Mezima-Wa wedding. During this time, although we all lived under one roof, Sam and Natalie could have no physical contact at all. They couldn't even sit at the same table to eat, though no one objected to them Skyping from their laptops between the rooms. At first, I felt glad to have Sam back to myself, whatever that means. But delicate marital matters demanded his—our—full attention: determining the agreed-upon number of children the couple would produce, for example, and the penalties should either side (not just the husband and wife but also their extended families) default. Natalie kindly pointed out that her family would naturally assume that as the husbandmother-to-be, I'd demand a number of children higher than Natalie could comfortably or safely bear—and only then would we negotiate.

Sometimes, passing by Sam's room, I'd see his face glowing into his computer screen. He'd smile and give a little wave. Then I realized that he was Skyping with Natalie—he didn't see me at all.

But he responded immediately to my messages.

"Two children is a nice number," I texted.

"Two is nothing. We can get more," he replied.

If I weren't divorced, it turned out, we could have commanded five or six children from poor Natalie. But Sam and Natalie agreed on three, and each of us signed the document that outlined specific ameliorations should Natalie prove infertile or unwilling to bear the planned number of offspring. I couldn't read the document, as it was written in Mezima-Wa. Sam read it aloud to me, translating as he went, his face adorably close to the page. Although I felt the document exerted a fair amount of pressure upon a young couple with student loans to repay, I signed my name on the line above the word *Husbandmother—Husbandmother,* the most beautiful concept in the Mezima-Wa language, Sam told me.

ENDING MY MARRIAGE had been like jumping from a beautiful tall building filled with people working and loving and laughing, a building illuminated against the darkness. I jumped and fell slowly, Alice-like, past each floor. I saw the various scenes of human contact and togetherness and knew that I could no longer live inside.

Marriage—the end, the loss of faith—is not something I'll recover from, financially or in messier ways. Recessions and housing crises are always good for my business, but I have a mortgage built for two and a son in college. To complicate matters, Bob isn't Sam's biological father, who was never in the picture, really. (That early encounter was brief and strangely productive, and it all took place during my junior year in Rome.) During the marital negotiation, Sam had asked me not to mention my impulsive youth. It was enough to say that Sam's father lived abroad.

When Sam announced that he and Natalie would be getting married in a traditional Mezima-Wa ceremony, I had three hundred dollars in my checking account and a Discover card I'd prophylactically cut in half. Circumstances compelled me to expand my practice—to bring more grief into my life.

Natalie's parents were better-off. Her mother had attended a Catholic high school among the Mezima-Wa, then, after the civil war and her move to the United States, put herself through community college and then through a master's program at Ohio State. She now directed an international nonprofit organization that did incredibly bold and dangerous work with child soldiers in war-torn countries. Natalie's father, Mondal-Wa, was an orthodontist. They spoke with pride about their Roth IRAs and 401(k)s (all of which were disclosed and enumerated on the marital document). Natalie was their only child.

Before we met, I felt confident that Natalie would warm to me. I've always been a favorite of girls, who see me as tough and independent and androgynously, fabulously feminist—probably because I am tall, single, and forty-five. But Natalie remained cool.

"Come, we live in America now," Natalie's mother, Fenn, told her daughter. Fenn explained to me that among the Mezima-Wa, divorced women lost all status. "It's a fate worse than death," she said, "though a small percentage of Mezima-Wa women still choose to leave husbands for the most serious reasons." These women lived together on the margins of the Mezima-Wa territory in a desperately poor but beautifully organized gift economy.

"All will be well," Fenn assured me, patting my arm. She picked up my hand and put my thumb into her mouth and held it there, looking sternly at the olive tree outside. This gesture of consolation is among the more endearing intimacies practiced among the Mezima-Wa. Before Natalie's parents arrived, I had seen Natalie do the same to Sam, and Sam reciprocate. The inside of Fenn's mouth was like another world—warm and dark and safe. We sat there for a long time—maybe fifteen minutes, my thumb in Fenn's mouth, and all was well.

Mondal-Wa was an attractive man, taller than I, with gorgeous, sleepy eyes. He admired my CD collection and shared my enthusiasm for Bill Evans, Miles Davis, Grace

Jones and the early Sting. He slept in Sam's bedroom; in fact, he slept in the same spot where Natalie had lately slept, next to my son, in the twin bed Sam had used since he was three. This was inviolate custom among the Mezima-Wa; the bride's father symbolically guarded the future husband, or guarded his daughter from the possible predations of the future husband. But Mondal-Wa's presence in my son's bed was not hostile or purely preventive, Sam assured me; it was also a chance for the father and husband to bond. Similarly, Natalie moved from my son's room into mine. She brought her pink ditty bag, her tampons, her incense, her secret birth control pills, her collection of bras from Victoria's Secret, her G-strings, her flannel pajama bottoms, her tank tops, her Haruki Murakami novel and her plastic basket of dirty laundry. She slept on the bed beside me.

Fenn slept on the floor. She claimed the red rag rug I'd stepped on first thing every morning and last thing every evening for the past fifteen years. At first, before Fenn explained its deeper cultural significance, this abasement horrified me. With one thing and another, raising my son, keeping up my practice and so on, the rug had probably gathered dust. But Fenn just shook it out the window that first night and smiled warmly through the sparkling motes. "Your dreams will reach me here," she said.

Fenn added that sleeping on the floor immediately beside the bed of the husbandmother was a privilege and even a pleasure. "It's a nice change for me," she confided. "I've slept next to Mondal-Wa nearly every night since our wedding—and he snores like a buffalo." I asked if she would like, at least, a yoga mat to lie on. She pursed her lips and then said, "Yes." When I found my old yoga mat—in the garden shed, of all places—she asked for a pillow (with feathers, if I had one). I felt we were making progress.

Natalie did not complain about sleeping next to me; in fact, she warmed slightly. We sometimes whispered for a few minutes after we put aside our reading (mine: "Experiential Connections Between Zen Buddhism and the Grieving Process"; Natalie's: Murakami) and turned out the lights. I asked Fenn if our whispering kept her awake, and she said, "The sound of your voices running together reminds me of my white-noise machine in St. Louis, which lulls me to sleep with the drumming of tropical rain."

THE MEZIMA-WA rarely drink spirits, although Sam and I went to some effort (williams-sonoma.com) to procure the specific seedpod, called *gamm,* grown on the northern plains of the peninsula and now threatened with extinction because of the loss of the *oruna,* a native songbird. One of the seedpods is ritually chewed by a matriarch (Fenn) and then spit into the calabash—the *sam*—to begin the fermenting process. The remaining pods are processed in the bathtub in the usual Mezima-Wa way, then added to the calabash, which is filled with water and held at room temperature for six days. (We used the bucket in which I brine our Thanksgiving turkey.) Some Mezima-Wa families stir the mash daily;

others allow the bubbles to rise to the surface undisturbed until the last day, when they whip it with a special spoon. (Fenn used a wire whisk.) The finished punch opens the voice of the Mezima-Wa, making possible the exchange of interfamilial information—medical and psychiatric secrets, for example—between the husbandmother and wifemother. (Mezima-Wa society is matrilineal.) These secrets are traditionally transmitted through song—actually a mimicking of the singsong cry of the *oruna*—under the heady influence of *gamm*. For the sake of clarity and more perfect communication, Fenn suggested that we speak in English, without attempting the specialized tones of the *oruna*—for which I felt grateful.

When the Mezima-Wa do imbibe, they do so intensely. We drank for the prescribed hours (seven) from one of my coffee mugs, the closest relic we could find to the traditional Mezima-Wa cup fired out of clay dredged from the Mezima Basin. Sam, of course, was exempted from the ritual. He used his free time to take care of a glitch in his student loan paperwork from his year among the Mezima-Wa (the bank had confused the University of Mezima-Wa with another accredited international university) and to watch old noir films in the den.

The *gamm* tasted yeasty and bitter, like the fermented oatmeal I once enjoyed at the wedding of my second cousin in Glasgow. I remember little of the night, except that the *gamm* kept returning. Among the Mezima-Wa, it's considered rude to "pass," or sip without gusto.

The alcoholic drink—the cup, the stickiness—reminded me unpleasantly of an uncle from my youth. But the experience advanced overall my relationship with Fenn and Mondal-Wa, who spoke of their courtship and early days together in the capital, and their affection for America—the International House of Pancakes, the Grand Canyon and the music of Cole Porter. They pressed gift after gift upon me—beautiful tunics in the traditional Mezima-Wa fabrics and colors (plant-based, mushroom-dyed), French-milled soaps, DVDs, a ninety-six-pack of toilet paper from Costco, a plastic hairbrush, a traditional tub-scraping shell and a large bottle of white vinegar. The couple told obliquely shocking stories of distant relatives, after which I revealed my own early struggles with dyslexia, and a discreet, partial narrative of Sam's quasi-father: his dedication to magazine journalism, our enduring friendship, his qualities of character, much-admired in Oslo.

After the drinking ceremony, Natalie and her parents took a ritual walk into the forest, where they built a small fire to symbolize the kindling of their new life among the husband and the husbandmother. I slept alone, exceptionally deeply, waking with a *gamm* hangover—not a headache, but, rather, a dinging pang in the area near my heart, a rousing sensation that I dimly recognized as something akin to a stirred libido, as if unfamiliar states of desire or appetite had been suddenly spirited up with a wire whisk. In fact, all the symptoms I had come to associate with midlife were gone.

Fenn, I found, had occupied the kitchen. She'd used my

Moroccan tagine to bake eggs with the strong cheese that the Mezima-Wa favor (any blue-veined variety will approximate it) and with parsley and the spices I recognized from Natalie's packets. She'd French-pressed coffee and sliced oranges. The CD player spun a trio in G minor by Schumann as Mondal-Wa read aloud the headlines from the *New York Times*. The crossword puzzle, folded into its quarter page, was almost complete.

Over breakfast, we discussed the plans for the wedding we'd agreed upon at the conclusion of the *gamm* ritual. The ceremony itself was to be held at the Mississippi River; the guests would form a receiving line leading up to the shore; any licensed person could officiate. Immediately following the vows (which Sam and Natalie had already written), the bride and groom would proceed through the gauntlet of their well-wishers directly into the river. They would swim in their wedding clothes, holding hands, some distance into the Mississippi, to symbolize the terminal depth of their union.

I realized only as it was ending how easily we'd slipped into a routine. Every day, Fenn borrowed a different pair of my shoes, "to walk in your way." Natalie disapproved of her mother's wearing the shoes of a divorcée. "But she is a child, very narrow," Fenn told me, stepping into a pair of tall leather boots. Every morning, before attempting the cross-word puzzle, Mondal-Wa went outside to greet the day, then jumped one hundred times on the trampoline in the yard, his face ablaze with pleasure, his perfect teeth gleaming.

The joy in Mondal-Wa's face as he jumped on the trampoline where Sam had spent so many hours of his youth—how can I speak of it? On this morning after the *gamm* ceremony, I ran down and joined him. I climbed up over the metal rim and studied his rhythms until I'd calibrated the perfect counterpoint, so that Mondal-Wa's landings on the trampoline lifted me higher, causing me to displace greater energy on landing and raise him higher still. We jounced dangerously, maniacally, until I lost my balance, and Mondal-Wa's hand reached out and pulled me back into the black circumference. I saw in his face real panic, real family feeling. After we settled, as if by instinct, I put his thumb—manicured, smooth—into my mouth. It seemed in the moment the most natural gesture in the world.

SAM AND NATALIE STOOD in the kitchen doorway together and announced that the wedding was off, due to an unbreachable rift between them. There was clearly no more to be said on the subject; Fenn and Natalie had both stopped speaking to me. I drove the family to the airport, leaving Sam in his room to process his grief. Mondal-Wa sat in the passenger seat beside me, shuffling through CDs and asking difficult, probing questions about the music of Amy Winehouse, until Fenn said, "Shh!" whereupon Mondal-Wa closed his beautiful eyes against me. Natalie and Fenn sat in back, Natalie's thumb firmly placed inside her mother's cheek. The curtain of formality hung between us, as if Fenn,

Mondal-Wa, Natalie, Sam and I had never shared those delightful intimacies made possible by the demands of family and strong tradition. I dropped them at the airport curb, with their Adrienne Vittadini luggage and couldn't even say *thank you.*

Sam sulked in his room for the rest of July, from which gloomy precinct he applied—successfully, it turned out—for a cultural fellowship to Gurinda.

Acknowledgments

Thanks to the editors of *AGNI, Gargoyle,* Fifty-Two Stories and *The Idaho Review,* where some of these stories first appeared. Thanks too to Anita Amirrezvani, Catherine Armsden, Randall Babtkis, Callie Babtkis, Eli Brown, Dorothy Cooke, Laurie Fox, Charlotte Gordon, Tess Holthe, Herb Kohl, Edie Meidav, Jordan Pavlin, Heidi Pitlor, Sarah Stone and Kate Walbert, for their insights and encouragement.

DAUGHTERS OF THE REVOLUTION

In 1968, a clerical mistake threatens the prestigious but cash-strapped Goode School in the small New England town of Cape Wilde. After a century of all-male, old-boy education, the school accidentally admits its first female student: Carole Faust, a brilliant, outspoken, fifteen-year-old black girl whose arrival will have both an immediate and long-term effect on the prep school and everyone in its orbit. There's the school's philandering headmaster, Goddard "God" Byrd, who had promised co-education "over his dead body" and who finds his syllabi full of dead white males and patriarchal tradition constantly challenged; there's EV, the daughter of God's widowed mistress who watches Carole's actions as she grows older with wide eyes and admiration; and, finally, there's Carole herself, who bears the singular challenge of being the First Girl in a world that's not quite ready to embrace her.

Fiction